Destruction

@EricMMrozek

@FreeEagleStu

www.ericmrozek.com

www.freeeaglestudios.com

DESTRUCTION

ERIC MROZEK

Free Eagle Studios
United States of America

Published by Free Eagle Studios, LLC.

www.freeeaglestudios.com

First Edition: August, 2015

ISBN: 978-0-9966707-0-8

eBook ISBN: 978-0-9966707-1-5

Table of Contents

PROLOGUE

THE STORM

Amatu sai sessitu amar.

We are who we choose to be.

- Almari Family Motto

CHAPTER ONE

20 Soltyde, 633 C.I.

The weather was calmer than I had expected today. I suppose that only added to the joy that I felt as I reached the age of majority along with my dear brother, Aegras. And yet, I do not think that any amount of preparation would render us perfectly ready for a meeting with the King and Queen of Callista. Apparently, Mother and Father had both placed the First Minister in their debts for a time and this was how things were made even once more.

"Now, remember that you must make three curtsies once you enter the Throne Room," Mother said, proper as she always is. "I have some business to attend to while your father takes you to the palace."

My twin is the silent one of the family, which was reflected in his incredible sense of calm as we passed two members of the Royal Rifles and entered the palace. I wondered why he seemed to be in such a state while my nerves had gotten the better of me, but the accursed telepath caught wind of my curiosity.

What is it this time? He followed Father as we whisked through one room and the next.

Are your nerves as quivery as mine, brother?

Not quite. We have been in places like this before. You should relax your mind.

Aegras has a way of finding the correct words at the right time, as the herald had just announced our arrival. For a moment, I found it odd that my father was exempt from making curtsies to the Royal House, but I suppose that he earned the right as a Captain and now it was our turn to do the same.

"We would like to wish you a happy birthday, Helisah and Aegras," the King said with a smile. He and the Queen fixed their gazes upon us even as they sat upon their thrones.

"Thank you, Your Majesties," we replied in unison.

"It is joyous for us to hear news of such great potential in our nation, especially those who come from a family of acclaimed service," the Queen said, shifting her piercing gaze between us. "For we tire of war and politics, from time to time."

"We are glad to have helped," I blushed. Perhaps in some ways, I am still a child at heart.

"And you can assist us even more before we feast tonight. What are you going to study in our college, Aegras?"

"Sorcery, Your Majesty. I hope to serve as my father does."

"The power that governs our world is entrusted only to those few who can use it justly. Tell us, do you plan to do the same due to your telepathic connection, Helisah?" the King asked.

I told His Majesty that I wished to engineer marvels, which was deemed to be a noble profession in the eyes of the King. I suppose that the approval of His Majesty could not compare to the shock that we felt when he gave us a gift of one hundred silver pieces each. What feats had my family wrought that could earn such favor?

• • •

The feast that followed could be considered the most natural of highs, but I am thankful to the mercenaries that tutored us at a young age because Aegras had other plans. The many dalliances that he has had outside of Elven-kind are typical of a young, crazed Callistan, but three people at once requires a little more discretion, to say the least.

I merely settled for one that night in the form of a young human Lieutenant of the Guard. He appeared so utterly bored by the proceedings that charming him was an easy feat. Luckily, the telepathic blockade had worked at the time and none of our own proceedings were ever known to anyone else.

I never knew the name of the man, but I also had never felt more alive than I did when we crashed into the nearest bedroom. I am truly thankful that the otherwise noisy party did not interfere with our affairs, for I am not sure that the honor of our family could hold up against two new adults who would apparently need to learn the meaning of privacy.

And yet, I am still not sure if dear Aegras is correct. Is becoming that crazed with primal desire a virtue that is at the core of ourselves, as he believes? Is it a place of utter madness? Is it somewhere in between those two states?

I have the feeling that I must dedicate a bit of time in the future to solving this riddle. I never deny myself the answers that

I seek and I see no reason to do so now, especially when Mother and Father have given me a set of new journals to record my misadventures in.

I shall have to make a note to purchase a packet of the incense that burned on the bedside. It was an intoxicating aroma of crushed cinnamon and flowers that I will not forget any time soon.

• • •

21 Soltyde, 633 C.I.

I must return to my books after my one day break, but I am not one to mind. Most of the free people of the world have been instilled with a love of learning from a young age, even if such a love may be taken in many different directions over the ages. I think that intelligence has more to do with applying knowledge, rather than spouting facts like a walking encyclopedia.

Several quadratics await me now.

• • •

22 Soltyde, 633 C.I.

Life in the city can be such a bore sometimes, but I think I should be grateful to be safe here as opposed to out in the wild, where none save the Royal Army and colonial expeditions dare to venture. One would think that the Dalarians would raise a storm about this matter due to their claims on certain lands, but it is said that their Republic operates on the Koronet and concerns itself with little else.

Mother actually took me to the Dalarian homeland for a

meeting with her friends at a time before I began to write. The only details that I could remember were the frigid cold of the deep winter and forests as far as the eye could see. If there had been anything else, I would have remembered it or made friends from there along the way, would I not?

• • •

23 Soltyde, 633 C.I.

It was brutally cold today and the cruel touch of nature was only made worse by the defense drills that the military ran in the city. The threats outside our door may be as fearsome as the wild drakes, but I do not think that corralling civilians into shelters will make a difference when a rival army is blasting at the walls. However, our Fiean allies are the only people that would be capable of such an attack and they have no reason to violate the peace pact that had been crafted after their revolution. The odds of them turning on us are about the same as if I ventured into the forest and encountered a walrus that could tell jokes.

• • •

24 Soltyde, 633 C.I.

As expected, no one had died in the previous night. Agosia has returned to normal and the impulse to do business has been picking up as of late. The New Year of our Independence is fast approaching and another celebration cannot hurt. To that end, our royal family is building up a grand lights show in the fields outside of the city to attract more tourists. Father mentioned that the outer walls need repairs, and the First Minister promised that tax revenue from the upcoming parties will go toward them.

I believe that I know what our Queen meant now. Most of the details of governance can bore you if you sit with them for too long. After a time, I think that I might need any distraction that may find a way to cross my path.

• • •

25 Soltyde, 633 C.I.

It appears as if the young Lieutenant that I shared a bed with has found me again in the market today. We ran into each other by happenstance in the bakery and an initially awkward conversation became an invitation to engage in a liaison once again. He took the opportunity to introduce himself as Khal. In spite of his initial bumble, he displayed an incredible confidence that I would continue to feel with his every word and movement. I must admit that his assertive nature and the thought that we should embark on a physical relationship was oddly intriguing.

I must admit that I am not certain about whether or not I have damaged my chance with Khal by asking him about his potential engagement in multiple relationships. The way his face contorted when I questioned him betrayed that he did not engage in such behavior. Is it not the unofficial creed of the Guard to fight and fuck as many people as possible?

I must quiz my dear Aegras on this. I hate to admit my faults, but he is more experienced in these matters than I am.

• • •

26 Soltyde, 633 C.I.

Well, it appears that the advice of my dear brother has paid off in my favor, if you could call bitter beer and sexualized card games the definition of the term. At the very least, Khal did not deny me what I felt on that first night and I have to applaud him for that.

I feel that I am inclined to see the good Lieutenant once more in the next few days. How could I dare pass up an offer to go and hear from musicians with a soldier such as he? It would besmirch the honor of my country!

● ● ●

27 Soltyde, 633 C.I.

I think that the chicken that was prepared for Khal and I ended up not agreeing with me. Thankfully, the medicine that Aegras retrieved quickly eased my pain. However, it seems that medicine and even magic cannot restore the regulated motions of the body just yet, as I spent much of today dry-heaving and barely able to keep down any food.

I suppose that I shall feel better tomorrow.

● ● ●

28 Soltyde, 633 C.I.

It is quite odd that a brief sickness can make me appreciate the times when I am at the fullest strength. The great resistance that Elves possess against bacteria is a remarkable factor in the near immortality of our race. The sicknesses that can kill us are usually so lethal that they burn out before spreading beyond our control. That is not to say that we cannot die of other causes. Even the great Elven Kings and Queens of Callista can die in battle.

Namalie of Arduth was a hero of mine when I was a child for this very reason, and I am constantly reminded of her when I see illness around me. She had gained great renown as the Mother of Medicine. I remember when she had come to our school and regaled us with tales of the horrors of the age before Callista and the Fiean Republic were founded all those years ago. It is such a shame that she died shortly after that lecture.

I understood from the moment that I heard the news that if ever I had to sacrifice myself, it should be to save another.

• • •

29 Soltyde, 633 C.I.

Khal was called away on a drill with his soldiers today, and I cannot help but feel torn between a sense of understanding and a sense of selfishness. It is such a good feeling to spend time with someone new, but I also cannot hold a grudge against someone who is expected to do their duty.

After all, what if I were in his shoes? I would definitely feel hurt and unwelcome if I had to spend time putting food on the table while others mocked and berated me for doing what I must. I forgave Mother and Father for that very same problem year after year since they had made every effort to be there for Aegras and me.

Absence helps one to reflect on their lives even better than usual, I suppose.

• • •

30 Soltyde, 633 C.I.

One day until the new year of our Independence and I am overcome with a desire to see the new lights show that our King and Queen have ordered. Indeed, it seems that others shared the enthusiasm of the residents of our capital, as the city swarmed with tourists and grandstanders from kilometers around. Father was tasked with watching the main gates of the city for a long while, only to be relieved by the safe return of Khal before the sun had set. My liaison was oddly silent about what had happened outside of the city, but it is better for everyone that these men and women could come home to their families on such a prestigious eve.

● ● ●

3 Hafelda, 634 C.I.

They are gone. All of them. Dead on the day of birth.

The openness of our Independence Day masked the movement of legendary monsters that had arisen from the great beyond. It all began as the Royal Light Show commenced outside of the city, revealing an approaching army of uncountable number. The behavior of the Horde betrayed their true origins. It was the resurgence of the Telurian Empire, which was once thought to be just a legendary collection of foes that were used to frighten gullible people.

We thought that we were safe inside the walls of the city and under the protection of a Guard of Elves, Dwarves and Humans, but it only took a few short hours before we were proven wrong. Aegras was present when the worst events had happened, relaying the hysteria to me as so many began to flee into the city. An insider had killed multiple guards and opened the Southern gate, much to the bewilderment of the defending army, but it was not just any traitor.

It was my Khal. The impossible man had doomed thousands to their deaths. For all my contemplation over his actions, I could not comprehend why he would commit such a vile act. Did he seek money? Power? The resolution of a blood feud?

Aegras put him down like a hog and quickly fled the area as a blood thirsty horde began to swarm into the city. Our own people tried to form a wall of gun fire, but the battle had quickly turned into a slaughter.

Meet at the fountain. He cast his thoughts out to all who would listen. With time, two of his friends made it. I could still smell the stench of a thousand corpses as we met in a panic.

"We need to leave," one of them screamed in fear. "They are killing everyone! We have to go!"

What about Mother and Father?! I shot to Aegras, failing to realize that he had begun to tremble in the face of the death and misery that rose all around us. A nearby explosion and several rising fires solicited a scream from us all, forcing Aegras to lead us away before the worst could happen. He remembered that Father had described a series of catacombs underneath the city that lead out into the wild. We had knives and sidearms, so it was better to face a bear than to end up dead in a city that was falling apart.

Aegras and I took the lead as our makeshift group moved deeper into the city. We were a bit removed from the fires and enemy projectiles, but the screams of the wounded and dying torture me even now. I cannot remove them from my mind.

And then, I saw him. A flash from the eyes of a cruel and

merciless killer. Father and Mother gathered a few brave beings together to make a stand, but the monster had easily cast them aside before he drove a dagger into the skull of Father.

And the voice. That horrible voice penetrated my mind as Father began to scream, soliciting a wail of my own as a part of his pain coursed through me.

I sense that you are nearby, son and daughter of the Almari bloodline. I will soon come for you both.

Thrakoth. That dark name was once only uttered in stories and legends, but his appearance in our home had been all too real as the monster cast Father aside like he was a piece of waste.

When we regained control of our own senses, Aegras and I found ourselves huddled against the wall of a nearby home. The friends of my brother were nowhere to be found, but matters were made even worse when a horde of Telurians spotted us. I wish I had known what to do at the time because they did not appear to want to kill us and be done. They wanted to send us to our graves slowly and painfully.

Luckily, that moment is also when the assassins came for us. Aegras and I stuck our fingers in our ears reflexively as a blast of arms rang out from above and many of the enemy began to fall to the earth. The shrouded figures then leaped off of several of the nearby buildings and stabbed the rest. I shall say with no uncertainty that we owe them our lives because of their prowess and efficiency in battle.

Why us? My family is respected, but we are not a special group of beings. Apparently, the Lord of the Telurians had known of our identities, yet we found protection from a source that I could not have foreseen. Our continuance through those dark hours threw guilt and conflict into the deepest recesses of my mind. We lived while so many others have died.

Little was said as the assassins led Aegras and I through the sewers and out into the wild. As we drew ever closer to safety, we would witness the Royal Citadel as it began to crumble. That single act would be of further detriment to our morale, but we were forced to move onward in the face of such a dark punishment.

● ● ●

CHAPTER TWO

6 Hafelda, 634 C.I.

The rush into the wild neared an end today and I have learned much about the supply network of these assassins. I dare not discuss much of it here, but most of the past five days was spent rushing between small caches of supplies in the forest and small towns. In the confusion of running from my burning home, I could not be certain of whether we were dodging Callistan or Telurian patrols, as our movements were erratic and not based on any particular time of day. One of the assassins explained that the level of trust that they had for outsiders in these dark hours was low and that they also did not want to fail in their mission to protect Aegras and me.

I feel that I must ask again. Why us? What did we do to deserve this?

• • •

7 Hafelda, 634 C.I.

It appears that the forward scouts of our tiny party have found what they were looking for. They were taking us across the border into the Fiean Republic and splitting us up. Aegras would go to the sorcerers of their group, while I would go to the main hideout. As their briefing progressed and they remained blissfully unaware of my eavesdropping, they also brought news of the outside world.

Agosia was not the only city that had fallen to the Telurians. A sizable portion of the Callistan military was besieged across every piece of what remained of our territory. Even though my people and her allies ruled the seas, it made no real difference to the people trapped in engagements hundreds of kilometers inland. Only a few choice coastal fortifications held out against the storm at hand, as whatever armies that attempted to besiege those estates were crushed under the might of a Callistan ship of the line.

That is a comforting thought. At this time, I will take all of the good news that I may get.

• • •

8 Hafelda, 634 C.I.

It was hard to say farewell to Aegras today, but some part of me knew that our training had to take priority over familial bonds for a time if we were to have revenge on the Telurians. My dear fellow telepath would still remain in my mind across hundreds of kilometers anyway, so it is not as if we were losing one another in the first place.

The assassins took me to a cabin nestled along a particularly pristine beach. It was fairly inconspicuous to all but the keenest of observers, especially since more assassins had secured the cabin and the surrounding wilderness. It was truly a sight to see.

In a departure from what I had seen so far, the leader of these assassins was not an elf, but a man. Upon first glance, he did not appear much different in stature than me, but he was far more dignified by age and expertise. A dozen years of scars had been strewn across his face. I presume that these wounds of war may also be found on the rest of his body, but I shall not pry my host for stories until he is willing.

"I am Melir. Melir Advardin," he said, outstretching a hand with a fatherly smile. Although I had never heard of the name before, it appeared that he wanted to be comforting first and a killer later, so I took his hand out of respect.

"Helisah Almari," I replied. "It is good to make your acquaintance."

"Oh, we already are acquainted. I remember you from when I visited your mother and father and you began to write in those journals of yours."

Before I could ask him what he knew about my family, he ushered me to a nearby chair and told me to sit down. I complied once more, as it seemed like Mister Advardin had already read my mind.

"Tell me. What do you know about your mother and father?" he asked, taking a seat across from me.

I told him the pieces of my family history that it seems a mere child would be familiar with. Father was a Captain. Mother was a Scholar and a Sorcerer. What more could there be than that?

"Before your mother had settled down and bore you and

your brother, she was an excellent spy," he remarked, leaning back in his chair. "I can only assume that her efforts to sabotage the Telurians have failed."

He looked like he was on the verge of crying for a moment there, but was it due to losing someone he knew or someone he loved? I could not be certain.

"And so, should the worst happen, your father and mother requested that I get you out. Now, what is it you would ask of me?" he said.

"These Telurians. They took everything from me and I want to fight back!" I said, letting my anger take hold as I remembered the screams and smells all over again.

"You wish to join the Raiders?"

At the very least, I now have a formal name for these assassins. It was one that was not even uttered in legends or tales, but I suppose that such writings would defeat the meaning and purpose of a secret organization.

"Yes," I told him, pushing my rage back under control.

"Then your training will commence tomorrow morning. Be ready for it."

At that moment, the face of a father figure was gone and the face of a cold man was left in place. He led me to my room and shut the door. It is here that I shall remain for the night.

I must rest now, for I feel that enduring tomorrow will not be such an easy feat.

● ● ●

9 Hafelda, 634 C.I.

The blast of cold water that greeted me in the morning proved my assertions were correct. A pair of Raiders were in the room and on my ass, snapping at me to get my thoroughly soaked body out of my thoroughly soaked cot and rise to greet the accursed weather outside. A torrential downpour pounded the ground outside and I was told that I was going to be training in ten minutes. They pushed me to gather up my new uniform, which was a customized version of what would be given to a Callistan Officer, and told me to get dressed in front of them, make my bed and eliminate my bodily waste before they kicked me out of the room.

I found myself seated in front of Melir after I scrounged together an order of fruit, cooked oats and meat from who knows where. He was as silent as could be, merely checking his pocket watch with one hand while counting down the minutes that I had to eat on the other. At the time, I was amazed at how I felt like I ate like a glutton, but I think that might have been the result of the regimented atmosphere.

With a minute to spare, the Raiders that had greeted me earlier in the morning returned to see that their Master had raised his thumb in approval. They ushered me up and out into the rain, quickly checking the light armament that they had donned before joining me.

"You will start running," the younger one, Fennigan, said. "I will tell you when to stop. Do you understand?"

I nodded and quickly broke out into the downpour and the

Raiders followed. My opening day was uneventful and boring in its focus on physical fitness, but little did I know what would greet me when the rain lifted and the sun shone once more.

• • •

My new overlords took me up to the cliff side overlooking the hideout and forced me to continue to strengthen my muscles. My entire body ached under the strain of constant exertion, but I struggled through the pain. For if I could not handle the pain of building myself up, how in the world could I ever face down Thrakoth and his hordes?

The exercises of this day were merely a dress rehearsal for the main event. My exhausted body was easy pickings for the Raiders to bind by the wrists and legs. Fennigan and his elder, Erudan, pulled me to my feet and dragged me to the edge of the cliff. I choked back a bit of fright as I observed the waves crashing against the sand. It was a terror that the Raiders had immediately sensed.

"How are you ever going to have your revenge if you fear Mother Nature herself?" Erudan whispered, mocking my squeamishness. "Are you a coward or are you going to fight?"

They were right. If I am going to survive this storm, then I would have to become fearless.

And so I did.

• • •

10 Hafelda, 634 C.I.

More physical training. More exercises. More everything. I managed to struggle through the soreness of my muscles and

Erudan and Fennigan issued me a dagger. I think that they will throw me out into the wild at some point, but it was not to be today.

Instead, sparring with the hands and legs was the focus of this day. Fennigan instructed me for much of the time that we spent in the sun. Father once taught me some simple tricks for the purposes of defending myself, but I was utterly destroyed in the first round of faux combat with the Raiders. Nearly every round of sparring resulted in my back hitting the dirt and an order to get back up. My brain had absorbed so much information that I had learned that speed and maneuverability were more important than strength. In time, this knowledge would be used to throw Fennigan to the earth.

"Outstanding, Helisah!" he groaned, catching his breath as I helped him to his feet. "Again!"

In another life, Fennigan probably would have been like some of the people that I had been with. He possessed that kind of charisma that would make most people – whether they be elf, human, or dwarf – happy to be around him and learn of the tales that comprised his brief life. I wonder if he will ever tell me a tale or if he shall focus only teaching the art of the kill.

And so, we fought round after round until nightfall. Fennigan was the superior fighter for much of that time, but this matter did not insult or demean me in any way. He would not be a master of his craft if I had been able to reverse most of the tricks that he had fielded against me.

● ● ●

11 Hafelda, 634 C.I.

I had a far easier time with the sword today, partly because very little damage was done using our hands. Erudan handed me a fencing blade and took me on in the place of Fennigan.

"You will sleep with this weapon at your side at all times," he said as he offered the blade to me. "You will treat it as if you would an extension of yourself, and it will become as if your hand is outstretched to strike at your enemies."

"Either that or chop them into bait for the wolves," I remarked, eliciting a smile from Erudan. It was good to know that the Raiders have a sense of humor, at the very least.

I cannot thank my Father enough for what he had taught me in my formative years, especially in those moments as I faced my first true opponent. It is hard to believe that he and Mother are gone.

Erudan saluted, I returned it, and we dueled with the passion and pride of what we had learned until we could no more.

• • •

12 Hafelda, 634 C.I.

I have only trained with the Raiders for a few days, but the skill and struggle of it all has caused me to respect the men that now dominated my life. I was caught off guard in the afternoon when Melir had seen fit to tutor me by seating me in front of a set of miniature soldiers. Apparently, the Raiders have served as generals in numerous battles. With the war now awaiting us to the east, they may do so again on behalf of the Fieans and Callistans.

"The first thing you must understand is that numbers mean very little in a battle, Helisah," Melir remarked, pointing out that I had two lines of infantry for every one of his. "You must learn to use every means at your disposal to break the will of the Telurians."

Memories of the disaster in the capital flooded my mind, but I began to look at them in a way that went beyond my own personal story. What if Khal had never opened the gate? What if panic had never ensued because the Callistan Army knew better? What if everything could have been different?

"Now, begin," Melir ordered. And so I moved forward a line of infantry and two cavalry pieces.

I asked Melir about the Raiders as we positioned our armies. The Raiders have been present in one form or another since before the founding of the United Kingdom itself. The name changes as each Head Master ascends, but the allegiances remain the same. The Raiders have always protected the concepts of democracy and individual governance and have never sworn allegiance to any government or national authority.

Two rolls of the die resulted in the disappearance of two of my lines of infantry under a cloud of imaginary cannon fire. I tried to reinforce from the reserves that I had, but it proved fruitless as a second hole opened up on my left flank. Luckily, that was easily countered by a blast of fake cannon fire of my own. In the end, this maneuver had been a distraction to draw attention away from the first gap. Before I knew what was happening, two cavalry units were swarming my positions. They were eventually taken down, but not before they had done fatal damage to my army.

"How did I beat you?" Melir asked, leaning backward in his chair. In spite of my defeat, I immediately knew what had happened. He had found every weakness in my strategy or made his own opportunities. He had made me think that he was going to attack one valuable point when he would actually hit another. It was as if he anticipated everything that I was going to do and then made it backfire on me.

I must do the same to Thrakoth.

• • •

13 Hafelda, 634 C.I.

One would think that a recent rain storm would cool the local area, but the first taste of the summer heat hit us today from the south and west. Although the sea pushed much of the heat inland, the unusual amount of sweat that accompanied my training ended up being most uncomfortable. Thankfully, Erudan and Fennigan decided to focus on firearms instead of more physical forms of combat.

"You are going to be working with the most common rifle in the world," Fennigan said, holding it up to me. "This is the Arduvai Repeater, Six Hundred Twenty Five."

He placed the Arduvai in my hands and instructed me on the basics. The safety. The metal cartridges. The tube magazine. How to mount a bayonet. It was harder to learn how to clean the weapon than to learn how to fire it, which is why these weapons revolutionized warfare when they were invented over one hundred years ago.

We spent the day shooting at various clay targets, moving or otherwise, until I had to reload eight rounds into the tube or swab out the barrel. The accuracy of the repeater was quite extraordinary, despite the drawback of having the firing mechanism jam once or twice. At the very least, the design of the weapon prevented it from exploding in my face from a misfire, as so many had done in the wars of the past.

Erudan and Melir attested to this fact when we had adjourned for dinner. As part of his years of service to the Raiders, Erudan would often steal information from firearms manufacturers and point out how their experiments often resulted in a barrel torn to shreds. Melir offered up a story in turn, revealing that many of his scars were from that exact same catastrophe happening to him on the battlefield many decades ago.

● ● ●

14 Hafelda, 634 C.I.

It is odd how sleeping with a firearm and a sword has become second nature to me after only a few days of training with them. It put my mind at ease so quickly that it seemed I was merely a frightened child only a few short weeks ago. I knew that these weapons might not save me if I were ever caught out in the open by a large horde, but I rapidly came to face the truth that my developing instincts and the Raiders that I would soon join would compensate for that particular weakness. I cannot walk alone.

With my rifle slung around my back and my sword in her sheath, I was treated to a lesson on intelligence gathering from

Melir and Erudan. Melir stated that although I was driven by vengeance, the need to gather information behind the Telurian lines would mean the difference between not only my own personal victory or defeat, but that of the wider world.

"How else would one exploit the battlefield and destroy an army that vastly outnumbers his own?" he said with a grin, rubbing salt into my wounded pride.

So, our dear chief assassin wants a fake war, does he? Well then, it is a war he shall have.

Since Erudan was a spy with far more recent field experience than Melir, he imparted information on gathering intelligence, administering medicine in combat, a look at battle plans and the Telurian language, and secrets that I shall not utter until Erudan meets his end.

I was assigned a few scrolls on the similarities and differences between Telurian and our common tongue, so I feel the need to continue my studies before I sleep. I begin language instruction tomorrow.

● ● ●

PART I

THE RAIDERS

Amatu kei lanin.

We are the shadows.

- The Motto of The Raiders

CHAPTER THREE

17 Areli, 635 C.I.

It has been well over a year since I started to learn from the Raiders and I feel that the exercises that Fennigan and Erudan are putting me through have reached their logical conclusion. In the time I have spent with these men, I have pushed the whole of my body and mind beyond my imagined limits. After making contact with Aegras for the second time, I am pleased to learn that he has done the same with the sorcerers. He did not reveal the breadth of his new powers, but seeing him summon protective shielding and what appears to be lightning is quite enough for me.

Today, Fennigan and Erudan engaged me simultaneously in a drill on fighting off multiple opponents that we have been doing for some time now. The focus was not to merely beat these men, for I had done that many times over. It was to master the improvisational skills that I would utilize in the field. Fennigan is a ruthless fighter when he is fully unleashed, but I find that a good kick to the stomach is as good a lesson as any for him.

Before we could be too injured by our dangerous escapades, Melir called us in out of the sticky air for an intelligence meeting. The usually pristine study that we use for our intelligence exercises was now a mess, littered with papers and maps from all over the Callistan and Fiean nations. The continental lines had been stable for the past week, but Callista was still only in control of forty percent of her former holdings on the mainland.

"Fennigan, would you say that Helisah is ready for battle?" Melir asked as we sat down.

"She is, Head Master," Fennigan replied. I must admit that I felt electrified by that compliment.

"Good. Now, for some good news. The Fiean Republic has officially achieved a state of total mobilization against the Telurian Empire."

Some luck at last. I knew it would take time for our beloved allies to mobilize, but I never knew that it would be this long. Perhaps our fortunes will finally change.

"First Minister Valiri has openly founded a government in exile in Nuveia with the Fiean Republic overseeing most of the specifics, which means that we are now in belligerent territory," Advardin continued, ushering his hands toward the ground. "Which leads me to your first assignment, Helisah."

Melir invited me to join him and face the map of Callista together, pointing out the town of Tulall, which is currently behind enemy lines.

"My spies report that the Telurians are sending supply convoys through Tulall," Melir stated, pointing out the main road running through the town.

He offered me a choice of whether or not I wish to seize or destroy the supplies in the wagon, but it was upon the condition that I must do it alone and leave no witnesses, lest the Telurians end up hunting down my new brothers and sisters.

"Fennigan will watch over you from afar," Advardin stated. "If you succeed, you shall have the right to call yourself a Raider."

I curtsied to him over that particular honor. It was not long before Fennigan and I gathered our equipment, bid farewell to the cabin and departed for places unknown.

● ● ●

21 Areli, 635 C.I.

The art of stealth and dodging patrols leaves little time to write, but it is especially true now that Fennigan and I are about a week away from Tulall. We have heard gun fire and cannon shot off in the distance at many points during our venture, but Fennigan assured me that those were merely armies in training, rather than the signals of death and destruction.

After all of this time and all of this misery, it is quite nice to experience peace and quiet, if only for a brief moment.

● ● ●

24 Areli, 635 C.I.

We have effectively crossed the front lines and are now making our way to Tulall. The lands under Telurian control have been quite peaceful since the downfall, but I fear that it is because the Telurians are unleashing some unimaginable horror upon the people left behind. I wonder if this is why Fennigan was sent along with me, for it is possible that the Raiders feared that I might snap upon seeing it and recklessly throw myself at the enemy. If that is the case, then I will not hold it against them for removing the emotional pressure to the situation, albeit at my own expense.

I have gotten to know Fennigan quite well over this little adventure of ours. He already feels like a lost brother or a friend I had not seen in years. Intriguingly, he was not forced to join the Raiders out of necessity, but was the grandchild of a Raider. Unfortunately, this association had turned him into a target for the enemies of the organization, which resulted in his recruitment after getting caught in a firefight between the Raiders and a faction of mercenaries that would eventually join the Telurian Army.

The skill at brawling that he had picked up while charged with his family bar kept him alive during those frightening hours, but his training would prove to be more useful as he survived year after year in the far east and kept the Telurians from invading.

I thanked him right then and there. Were it not for his skill and willingness to fight, Aegras and I probably would have died in the bonfire that our home became, rather than living and being able to fight back now.

I assume that is what Mother meant when she spoke at length about the intertwining nature of all sentient life. Maybe it was an unintentional hint about who she really was at heart, but I took it as more of a moral lesson. Our actions, for good or ill, will cascade through history whether we want them to or not.

• • •

26 Areli, 635 C.I.

Tulall is in sight. Fennigan entered the town in the morning to scout for any potential threats, but he has ordered me to stay behind and keep watch for the convoy that I will attack. It has been approximately eighteen hours since he departed and I am starting to become worried for him. I am distracted by the cold that has only served to worsen my mood. I cannot start a fire for fear of being discovered and, were it not for the movements of the Telurians, I would have nothing but eating and shivering to contend with.

My biggest fear is falling asleep, so I am mumbling songs to myself from another time and another life.

You are damned, Thrakoth.

• • •

27 Areli, 635 C.I.

I am relieved to see Fennigan once more. Apparently, he was delayed by a dramatic increase in Telurian security as a resistance movement has taken root in the occupied territories. There was an attack inside the makeshift headquarters of the Telurian military and the enemy has declared a state of martial law in response. There is a mass prison camp that is being constructed inside the town and the residents of Tulall are being taken in small numbers. Males. Females. Children. The monsters are growing indiscriminate with their blood rage.

I was supposed to carry out the task of a simple convoy raid, but I believe that our situation has changed. If we leave Tulall behind, her citizens will likely die. If we free them from their camp and help them seize their lives back, it probably will not be long before the Telurians learn of the victory and burn Tulall to the earth.

Neither Fennigan nor I could make peace with these paths, so we had created one of our own. The city must be evacuated.

"Agreed," Fennigan said as he kept watch on the road. "You can seize the supplies that are coming this way and we will get the Callistans on our side. I will watch over you and stop any surprises from interfering with your raid."

• • •

Our plan had been set in motion much earlier than expected as the convoy had passed our way within three hours of the return of Fennigan. As my comrade took his perch on the branch of a nearby tree, I began to stalk the enemy, understand their movements and gather information before the strike.

"Keep that weapon away from the center wagon or the General will have your heads!" a man-at-arms shouted, shoving the rifle of a subordinate out of the way.

Ammunition. Weapons. Explosives. Any of these could have ruined my day if I did not know better. Thanks be to my heroes for developing the virtue of patience within me.

"Do you think we will have some of that sweet, salted ham when we get to the lines?" a Telurian elf asked of his dwarven comrade.

"Aye," the dwarf replied. "Get your first taste of Callistan blood and we will have all the rations we want."

I felt no sympathy for the Telurians as I circled to the back of the convoy. It shall be said for posterity that I felt good when I began to abduct them from the road and put an end to their lives. These feelings were not out of blood lust, for that was their domain. Instead, I felt relief as I emerged from the bushes and eliminated my foes.

It felt quite miraculous to see that no one was the wiser as I stabbed each Telurian in the neck and dragged them into the wilderness. They might have caught me had they merely paid attention to their surroundings, but my ability to remain unseen was a testament to how disciplined the Raiders had trained me to be. I felt particularly tense as I climbed into each wagon and took the life of the drivers, but I managed to remember my training even as I grappled with all of the possible ways that I might fail. Thankfully, it seemed as if the horses were on my side as well, for they never whinnied in fright at my presence or scampered off the road as I halted each wagon and cut them loose.

I am a truly lucky female.

● ● ●

28 Areli, 635 C.I.

We took stock of the spoils that the enemy had left for us. According to Fennigan, there was enough food to sustain all of the potential evacuees for a few days, but such good news was mitigated by the fact that the weaponry available to us consisted mostly of artillery rounds, rather than the small arms that we would truly need.

What few rifles and sidearms we recovered were largely of poor quality. I took a newly designed repeating sidearm for my own, but every other armament was a poor copy of Callistan designs. The similarities lead me to believe that a fellow may have betrayed us, but the result of their efforts leads me to believe that the art of making great machines can only be imitated when one does not master that craft.

We have a limited window of opportunity before the Telurians notice their missing supplies, so Fennigan and I will attack tomorrow.

• • •

29 Areli, 635 C.I.

The execution of several insurgents created the means for our strike. Dozens of prisoners were forced to look upon the hastily constructed gallows that the Telurians had built, but we had only uncovered their dark predicament after the first six prisoners had been executed. From a barren rooftop fifty meters from the gallows, we observed the movements of the Telurians and their captives with relative ease. Fennigan and I still feel the burning rage that coursed through our veins when we beheld the lifeless corpses that hung over the crowd.

I knew from the start that I may not be able to save every being, for that is the very nature and darkness of war. Yet I think that this was the first moment that Fennigan and I were completely attuned to one another. The deaths of our kindred were the charge that drove us forward with unnatural speed as another six inmates ascended to the gallows, ignoring the weight of the many weapons that we carried and the wide array of monsters that would rise to greet us.

I rushed down to the street as Fennigan began to pick off the overlooking guards like flies. As blade and flesh met on the rooftops, I pushed my way through the crowd of my frightened brethren to the gallows themselves. The Telurians paid the crowd and me no mind, for they were focused on securing the condemned. The nooses were tied and the executioner flipped the lever, but it was all for naught as six shots rang out from above, destroying the ropes that would have killed on any other day.

Hysteria took hold of friend and foe alike as I blasted my way through the throng of Telurians guarding my people. Some of my brethren took the opportunity to flee, but many more stayed and struggled with the Telurians for rifle and sword. As they did so, I set those captives free and armed them with the weapons that they would need. Very little was said as Telurian and Callistan alike fell during the onslaught, but the battle had not come to favor the Telurians. Skilled warriors of each race and gender rallied to destroy the oppressing army. In due time, our superior numbers overwhelmed the enemy and began to push them away.

I would never tell Melir that this was the case, of course.

Fennigan would eventually join me on the ground as the fight went our way, guarding my back against all of the dangerous brutes that Thrakoth could muster. He switched from knife to firearm and back again with such a grace and flow that numerous bands of the enemy fell before him. I was not quite as lucky. Although I had mastered his teachings and learned all that I could, I could not foresee the graze of a sword as it slit my cheek.

The offending Telurian threw me up against the steps of the gallows and throttled me. I cried out in pain, but my struggle against him was nothing that a kick to the genitalia and an eventual intervention by Fennigan could not solve. He ripped the enemy away from me, stabbed his neck multiple times and tossed him aside. As I rose to my feet, I knew that any sentiment between Fennigan and I would be expressed by the language of our bodies.

After all, why should we have wasted our time with a simple expression of thanks when there was a battle to win?

The conflict settled down with the raiding of the prison camp and the slaughter of every Telurian in it. No Telurian was spared the wrath of the citizens of Tulall, but whatever dark force that Thrakoth had instilled in them had taught these monsters to never surrender in the first place.

If only they had realized their folly. If only.

• • •

31 Areli, 635 C.I.

It took longer than Fennigan and I had anticipated to get back on the road, but that was due to political squabbling among the leaders of Tulall more than any other factor. Some had advocated that the town should take a stand and use the supplies stored in the Telurian camps to strike back at the enemy, but Fennigan and I swiftly changed the tone of the conversation.

We were brought forward for questioning by the locals and made our account of the swarm tactics of the many Telurian battalions that we thought would soon surround them.

"And what would you have us do?" A local man blurted

aloud. "Run? Flee for our lives while they burn the nation?"

"No," I cut in, standing with Fennigan. "We are saying that if you wish to survive this war, you should meet with either our military or the Fieans and fight that way."

The news of the Fieans entering the war was enough to convince all but a few stragglers to head for the front. These few that we were to leave behind were veteran soldiers in their own right and they felt that this war could be better served by the formation of a resistance movement. Although I thought it to be absurd at first, I realize now that they would likely understand the need to stay on the move and build up strength lest they be overwhelmed by the Telurians. And along the way, the opportunity to sabotage, kill and ultimately ruin the power of Thrakoth would save more lives from falling to the hordes.

We are four days away from the front with several hundred people marching at our backs. As we move on our path, I hope that we are not found out by the enemy. If they were to come upon our trail, I fear that disaster would befall us all.

• • •

CHAPTER FOUR

2 Jaudil, 635 C.I.

I tire of the delays in our journey westward, but Fennigan believed that the speed of our march would grow to be even over a long span of time. Our movements were greatly constricted as we drew closer to the Telurian patrols that had retreated since we had last seen of them. Fennigan and I were uncertain of whether or not this retreat was to draw our armed brethren into a trap or if the allies had pushed them back. In either case, the fear of being discovered left us with no time to solve such a riddle.

Out of all the problems that had stymied our journey, the disease that several of the refugees had left Tulall with was by far the worst. I am not surprised to witness the emergence of this contagion, as the putrid conditions that Tulall had fallen into are known to provide a breeding ground for all sorts of horrors. Luckily, this particular trouble was of small consequence compared to others, consisting of an upset stomach, a flowing nose, and pain that radiates throughout the body.

We could do little for them but offer water and help them along the road, but these small deeds have helped to sustain those that have accompanied us. I am very grateful that none of the afflicted have died.

• • •

6 Jaudil, 635 C.I.

With the receding of our traveling disease and the crossing of the front lines, our company has disbanded. We were left to resume our own journey back to Melir and his home. It is good to be back in safe territory after such dangerous games behind the lines of the enemy, but I think that I shall have little time to rest before I am sent out again. Fennigan and Erudan would leave me to sort out the enemy on my own, which instilled in me with a fear of the unknown and a certain measure of happiness. I was finally trusted and belonged somewhere after such a long time. Fennigan attested to this notion as we moved onward toward the coast.

"You are one of us now and the road will not be easy," he said, patting me on the back. "I know you will do your best to make things right."

Aegras began to probe my mind and revealed his location to me. I had expected my dear brother to be in a faraway library, but he was on the shore and in the presence of Melir.

It is good to hear that you are safe, Helisah. I could feel the burst of relief, somewhat akin to a telepathic embrace.

It is good to hear from you as well, Aegras. I feared that you would burn your eyebrows off with your newly acquired lightning powers. I thought, earning a laugh.

It is good to be almost home.

• • •

8 Jaudil, 635 C.I.

Two days of rest and a healthy dose of combat training were just what Aegras and I needed to calm our nerves. After my morning dash through the trees, I spent much of the day blasting targets with a repeater while Aegras electrocuted and burned them. My brother had spent much of his training and the entirety of his first raid under the telepathic block, so we recounted our adventures to one another with minor embellishments here and there.

Whereas my raid was more overt and bombastic, Aegras had dealt the Telurians a blow by stealing secrets. As he recounted his personal battles, I marveled at how perceptive Melir was in selecting the right raid for the right person. He sent Aegras into a situation in Arathia that required the employment of an equal dose of fighting and fucking just to survive, which appeared to be the perfect fit for my dear old telepath!

The Telurians seized Arathia not long after the fall of the capital. According to Aegras, it has since become a command center for the northern battalions of the enemy. The situation inside the city was far different than that of Tulall. Several of the locals were collaborating with the Telurians. Aegras was charged with getting personal with the enemy and making their fates look like accidents, which he accomplished with glee while remaining completely invisible to the conquerors.

● ● ●

The time spent with Aegras was enough for Melir to gather together the nearest Raiders and prepare a small celebration for our entrance into the brotherhood. It was a surprise to see the assembly as Aegras and I entered the cabin at nightfall. It was far removed from what I was used to in my former life, but I think that the healthy dosage of ale and a sense of family more than made up the difference.

Melir appeared before the crowd to the bows of every Raider, beckoning us forward with a quiet wave of his hand. Aegras and I could sense that every eye turned to the three of us out of acceptance, rather than negativity or fear. We took our place in front of Melir and stood with dignity as the room became silent.

"Every Raider here has to take our most solemn vow to protect all that we care about and all that we stand for," Melir said, his voice booming so that all could hear. "And now, it is time to welcome Aegras and Helisah Almari into the fold to help carry us into the future. Aegras and Helisah Almari, be mindful. The vow that each of you will make is not to be taken lightly and shall be carried with you until the day that you die. Are you prepared to join us?"

"I am," Aegras and I said, he after I.

"Fellow Raiders, I ask that you join in welcoming your new brother and sister by recounting your own vows," Melir said, taking a small book from a nearby table and opening it. "Aegras and Helisah, raise your right hand and respond with the words, 'I do.'"

We raised our hands as commanded, and every other Raider in the room did likewise out of solidarity.

"Do you pledge to uphold the rights of all people born on this earth to choose their own destiny?" Melir asked, looking between the two of us.

"I do," we said, one after the other.

"Do you pledge to uphold the ideals and principles of democracy in all her forms against destruction, whether from outside forces or from within?"

"I do."

"Do you pledge to uphold the secrecy and strength of this order by any means necessary from enemies both outside and within?"

"I do."

"Do you pledge to aid the oppressed of our world by any means necessary?"

"I do."

"And finally, do you pledge to never turn your weapons – whether they be words, blades, or firearms – on the undeserving, the innocent, and all others that you shall defend?"

"I do."

"Welcome, Helisah and Aegras," Melir finished, closing his book. "And now, we shall celebrate with good food, good ale and our ever larger family."

The rest of the Raiders cheered, which brought me to tears out of great joy. Now more than ever, I feel that my brother and I have reclaimed a piece of our home from the darkness. And I will be accursed if I let Thrakoth or any of his servants take this measure of comfort from us.

• • •

9 Jaudil, 635 C.I.

After a day of celebration, Aegras and I are parted once more. Melir did not say much about where my brother was to be assigned, but the Raiders and the Fiean government have lost contact with an allied expedition that had been sent northwest to an unexplored island. It was up to Aegras to pick up the pace in the absence of the now presumed dead Callistans and Fieans in the war against Thrakoth.

Well after Aegras had departed, Melir called me into his chambers to discuss the dangers that await me on my new assignment. The work is far more difficult than I had anticipated. I have to get close to a Telurian Marshal that the Raiders found in the central portion of the Telurian line. In addition, Melir levied a special circumstance upon me.

"Do not attempt to liberate Falde," Melir warned, his voice as stern as could be. "Tulall was filled with militia and guards that were no spy hunters. This is a command center for the enemy. You will die if you prematurely reveal yourself."

"How am I to get to my target?" I asked, peering over a map of Falde.

"Laktan prefers to pick female servants from both the local population and his army to fulfill his sexual appetite. Therefore, we have retrieved this for you."

Melir grabbed a box from the floor, placed it on his desk and opened it. It was a Telurian dress, complete with a thigh holster for a dagger.

"We made a few slight modifications that will help one of our assets to recognize you, but do not hesitate to kill her if she turns on you," Melir said, pointing to the green and golden brooch on the dress.

"Understood."

"Any questions?"

"None."

"Then, you are free to go. You depart tomorrow."

I turned to leave, but Melir spoke once more.

"And Helisah," he said.

"Yes?" I turned back to him.

"Do not take anything that could identify you, especially not your journals."

It appears that I must say goodbye to writing for a week or two. I may not remember many details when I return, but I have never known myself to be stupid or headstrong enough to risk my life for the sake of posterity and I am not about to become such an elf.

● ● ●

25 Jaudil, 635 C.I.

Where do I begin?

The Callistan Army pushed back the Telurians in several key locales, which made my crossing of the front a longer journey than I had anticipated. My bow, rifle and dagger kept me fed through the ride across Callista, but the wildly swinging weather patterns took a great toll on my push. The heat and the rain forced me to diverge from the road and move from forest to forest, emerging only to check the roads and track where I had gone.

Falde was one of the major trading posts of Callista due to her central location and favored status among merchants traveling from every direction, save for the Telurians. One can imagine my surprise when I found that the Telurians did not ransack the town and steal her riches for themselves. Indeed, the Telurians have established themselves as the new overlords, allowing traders from the Dalarian Republic, the Kingdom of Northern Arthan and the Abuzian Confederation to share their goods while taking the taxes to fuel their war machine.

I wonder if they knew about the kind of monsters they were supporting, but it is possible that they do not care. Money is sometimes a more powerful motivator than conscience.

The similar appearance and language of the Dalarians to the allied nations had made it easy for me to slip into Falde unnoticed. I discarded my rifle and paid a Dalarian merchant to bring me in on his wagon. I am still in awe of how easy it was to hide even as we crossed multiple Telurian stations on our way into the stomach of the beast, but I had not known of these conditions at that time.

I still think that they would have been more paranoid after our exploits at Tulall. Thrakoth must have a larger plot in play to sledgehammer his opposition into ruin. It seems quite odd and lacking in sense.

That is not to say that Falde was not a challenge, for I would be arrogant to state otherwise, but I am going to eat my dinner and get some rest before I record that absurd venture.

• • •

26 Jaudil, 635 C.I.

My movements into the home of Marshal Laktan were no easy feat, for I was watched from the moment I set foot in the city. While the city was at peace and as cosmopolitan as it could be, the presence of the Telurian Army made me watch my steps carefully, for anything out of the ordinary would result in the stamping of my own execution order.

Luckily, the Telurian noose loosened when I entered the Dark Horse Tavern and Inn. The famous Callistan brewery had been repossessed after the fall and sold to a Dalarian for several thousand Imperial Maldrounis, and it was said that the entire city had fallen under the same policy. There was no feeling of malice in the place and it was believed among the many drunkards and whores that the Telurians wanted to keep the places where people could be forgetful and happy intact.

The jarring shift in tone from the attempted genocide at Tulall reflected a far more careful and feared Marshal. The tavern grew silent when he entered with his two guards, but no one began to beg for their lives like a miserable wretch.

Laktan was respectful of the people under his rule, which made me more worried about confronting him than anything else. Any old fool can kill out of rage or a sick sense of ownership over a subject, but it takes a master of the psyche to slowly turn someone to your side. In time, they might have cheered him as a liberator were it not for his soft spots for beer and the feminine touch.

I was downing a raspberry ale when the Marshal approached me. He would have been oddly charming had he been sober. Liquor has the ability to make us all appear far less articulate than we actually are.

"Hello, there," Laktan said. "I am the Marshal in this... town, this town."

"How did you know that I was new in town?" I asked, putting my ale down.

"You are not as dirty as the rest of us."

What a refined man, no? For a time, I could hardly believe that I was sent to kill this man that was wiggling his fingers around and thinking that he was about to swoop me up and fuck me. Unluckily for him, this was not some normal day where I could just reject his sloppy attempt at a conquest. The moment that he set foot in the tavern was the moment that I knew that I would be going home with him by any means necessary.

"I bet you would like to test that idea out, would you not?"

"Well, I do not know," he hiccuped, covering his mouth briefly. "I doubt that such a clean and proper elf could handle me... with your frilly hair and your... oh, everyone, look at me, I am a Telurian and I am really well behaved!"

I like to be honest when I write about my encounters, so here is a small truth that I must admit. That bastard made me laugh exuberantly at that. I looked around briefly and it seemed like some of the local patrons were about to shit themselves in fear, but Laktan was focused entirely upon me.

"Sorry, you are too funny," I said with a smile. "I am

Amariah."

"Field Marshal Laktan," he said, kissing my hand.

"A pleasure. I almost forgot to ask this of you. Did you have your eyebrows colored recently?"

"I may have forgotten to wipe off the war paint from a drill yesterday," Laktan grinned, allowing a small glimpse at his mind. "Does it please the lady?"

"I am not quite sure. I think that you should close your eyes and let me see."

He did, opening the way for me to kiss him to the astonishment of certain onlookers. After a short while, Laktan, his escort and I were out of the Dark Horse and on the way to his residence.

I wish I could say that I fucked him to death and was done with this particular journey, but the situation on the inside was as dangerous as Melir had anticipated. On the negative side, my movements while in the company of the Marshal would be watched as if this were merely another public place and I was a suspicious subject.

On the positive side, it was good to know that such elite Telurian soldiers could never and would never prevent the screams that would emanate from the bedroom that night.

● ● ●

CHAPTER FIVE

27 Jaudil, 635 C.I.

The residence was quite open and quite secure, so much of the day after I bedded Laktan was spent in the company of the few servants and guards that he had assigned for his new mistress. Neither the Marshal nor his minions had discovered my dagger, which only added to my thought that having every single one of my needs looked after was both a blessing and a curse. I had earned the trust of the Marshal, yet I could not converse with any being without being overheard by spies.

That was not a problem when it came to ordering breakfast, but it could have become a disaster when the eyes of a servant went wide at the sight of my brooch. I never saw her again after that morning, but I can only assume that she disappeared into an ocean of money that Melir had provided for her. I still ponder what happened to her, but I could not focus on such matters as my plan would eventually require the implication of another. The best candidate would be someone who shared the predilection of Laktan for erotic adventure.

One of the Lieutenants of the Elite Guard of Laktan – Elliah was her name – would open the door for my mission to commence, but the matter would require a bit of convincing and intelligence gathering before she would join me. She was very friendly and open to meeting the new conquests of her superior officer, but I think that she focused upon her duty above any other notion.

Now that I think about the walk that Elliah and I took through Falde, I am still thinking of whether I misjudged the Telurians. Every action that they had taken in combating what they described as the Callistan and Fiean menace was described as an act that was righteous and pure, but to an end that only Thrakoth knew.

"Ours is not to question, but to serve the man that has never steered us wrong," Elliah said. Initially, I dismissed this as propaganda and brainwashing, for no one could truly be without imperfection, could they?

"I think that we all aim to serve as best as we can, but surely even our Lord would benefit from differing points of view, no?" I countered.

"I do not concern myself with the affairs of our Lord. The matters of my Marshal are my first and only means of service. I serve him. He serves the Lord."

"And has such valiant service led to just rewards for our noble Marshal?"

"Yes and no. He normally receives regular promotions and rewards, but I do not believe that he did after overthrowing the Callistan capital."

I struggled to restrain myself from flashing anger or any

sort of emotion at a casual musing about the massacre that had destroyed my life and the lives of so many others. Fuck their cause and fuck their desire for glory. I resolved that both of them would die that night by my hand.

"Then perhaps we can reward him ourselves," I said, pawing at Elliah. "I know a few techniques that will make this night unforgettable."

"For whom?" Elliah asked, her interest piqued.

Who did she think?

• • •

All of the pieces were in place for my strike as I cajoled the Marshal to go to his chambers that night. As the Marshal and I entered his bedroom, Elliah was already acquainted with the bed and exploring her own body with great enthusiasm.

"And what is this?" Laktan said, his eyes wide with wonder as Elliah moaned. "Have you ensnared one of my captains already, Amariah?"

"This is my gift to you," I said, planting a kiss on his shoulder. "Rumor has it that you deserve a reward for your valor."

We undressed each other with incredible haste and were off to the chase as Laktan paid attention to Elliah and me in equal measure. We were generous to each other, but Elliah needed more time to open up to the touch of her Master than I did. All the while, I masked my revulsion at these monsters by participating in any escapade that Laktan wished of me, which forced my sexual high after a brief while. Elliah and Laktan had begun to reach their own pinnacles of ecstasy. Their focus on gratification would be their undoing. I opened up my nearby chest of drawers, withdrew my dagger and ended their lives even as I stood as nude as could be.

There was no time to reflect on what I had done. The spilling of Telurian blood marked the beginning of my efforts to plot an escape. I cleaned myself with the bowl of water that had been left on my dresser and wiped any trace of my presence from the room. I only had a few hours before the enemy would discover what had happened, so I planted the dagger in the hand of Elliah before dressing and slipping out.

Two guards greeted me with a nod, stepping aside as I attached my brooch to my dress and donned a pair of fine leather gloves.

"The Marshal is quite indisposed at the moment," I said, waving them away. "It would be best not to disturb him until morning."

I must have neglected to completely clean my body, for the guards noticed that the blood of my enemies had dotted my right arm just as I had turned away.

"Stop!" They said, drawing their long swords as I broke out into a sprint. One followed after me while the other entered the bedroom of Laktan and emerged with new cries.

"Assassin! Assassin!" she screamed, moving off in another direction. "Awaken! The Marshal has been murdered!"

For the first time since the fall of Agosia, I feared for my life as guards swarmed after me, but that only drove me forward as my veins were overwhelmed with adrenaline. I entered the kitchen, dove through the back door of the residence and sprinted out into the darkness of Falde. Although the Elite Guard of Laktan had spewed forth from the residence like water from a bubbling geyser, shots from rifle and pistol alike failed to stop my egress as I weaved my way through the streets. The whole city seemed to awaken at the sound of battle, yet the actions of the enemy were all for naught as I liberated a horse and galloped into the wild.

And that is all I have to say. I wish I had taken better care not to make a scene, for not even Melir knew what had happened in Falde after word of the assassination and my hasty escape had spread far and wide.

• • •

28 Jaudil, 635 C.I.

"So, was revenge all that you thought it would be?"

I could not help but ponder the words of Melir even as we discussed how Aegras and I were to be sent to the Fieans for a time. My killing of Laktan and Elliah helped me to avoid the nightmares and sleep well for the first time in a great while. I dreamed of sitting in a tended garden and taking in the sun. None of these feelings would bring back the world that we have lost, but it felt good to think of such simple things until Melir opted to purge any notion of petty revenge from my mind.

Melir might be an incredibly wise man, but the way that he withholds half of the truth and half of the lesson is nagging at the back of my mind. Does he do all of these things with every recent addition to his flock, or is it confined to me?

On the case of the Fieans, Aegras and I are to meet with

the representatives of the Republican Government and First Minister Valiri to discuss the course of the war. It has come to the attention of Melir that there are pockets opening up in the Telurian line. From his point of view, the Callistan and Fiean Intelligence Services know far more about the movements of Thrakoth and the aftermath of my recent quests than we do. Therefore, Melir thought that a break from the war would serve the two of us well, but would also aid in warding off the complete and utter doom of the free people who are fighting in this war.

"I have a feeling that your dear brother has already intercepted what we have said here today," Melir said with a grin. "Tell him to make haste."

I have heard him, Helisah. Aegras communicated almost immediately, letting me see through his eyes as he galloped across the land. *Tell him that I am on my way north now.*

"Oh, he heard your words," I replied, prompting Melir to scratch his head. "He is on his way here as we speak."

"How in the name of sanity do you get any privacy?" Melir wondered aloud. "You must drive each other mad."

You do not know the half of it. Aegras thought with a chuckle, apparently forgetting that he cannot communicate through me.

Oi, stop it, you! I threw back at him in faux outrage.

"Very, very carefully," I told Melir. "I take my leave, Head Master."

I look forward to this assignment, for it appears that my daft old telepath might need a stern talking to... or so I tell people in jest. In reality, the fact that Aegras has more of an ability to act childishly than me is something that I envy, especially when I think of how pointless life would be if every being were to turn into a mindless drone.

Thank you for reminding me why we are fighting, Aegras. I hope I never forget.

• • •

31 Jaudil, 635 C.I.

The journey south and west into the Fiean Republic was predictable, especially when I came ever closer to the capital, Nuveia. The course of the war pushed the Fieans to turn their largest city into the most impregnable fortress on the planet, largely out of their fear that the sudden sack of Callista would be repeated in every corner of the known world.

"This is for your protection as well as ours," the Fiean Guards said as they ushered me to the front of the line and patted me down. "Remember that the carrying of concealed weapons is severely restricted in Nuveia to all but trusted members of the Fiean or Callistan authorities."

The guardians of Nuveia eventually found the dagger that I had used to slay Elliah and Laktan holstered on my left leg, which forced them to pull me aside for questioning until Aegras intervened on my behalf. It was explained away with a half-hearted apology that Fiean Intelligence had grown increasingly worried about Telurian threats against their capital and, therefore, every security measure imaginable was authorized by the Fiean Chancellor and First Minister to combat the enemy.

To the benefit of my patience and sanity, Aegras had opened Nuveia to me and a pair of soldiers were there to escort us to the diplomatic apartments near the Residence of the Fiean Chancellor and the Legislature. Ever more bureaucrats from both of the allied governments were crossing this way and that in a hustle as we placed our horses in the care of the stablehands. It was interesting to see that the Fieans lived in absurd levels of luxury. Marble floors and impeccably designed statues and paintings greeted Aegras and me as we made our way to our separate bedrooms and put away our clothing and supplies.

"We are to see First Minister Valiri with immediate haste, Helisah," my dear old telepath said, much to my dismay. "The Fieans are planning a feast for their ambassadors and the Callistan government, so we can start gathering information tomorrow night."

My brother took his leave so that I could have enough time to write and be settled in, but I feel that this time away from me has come to an end.

● ● ●

The sight of First Minister Valiri after several months in the wild was most welcome, although he could pay little attention to us at the time. Emissaries and Ministers from the Callistan and Fiean realms alike would move in and out of the room in mere moments and beg for his attention even as our names were heralded. On first glance, it appeared as if the First Minister had gotten little sleep since the downfall of our homeland.

"Ah, Aegras, Helisah, it is good to see you both," the First

Minister said as we approached. "I apologize for such a hasty meeting, but I felt it necessary since it has come to my understanding that you are now fighting behind the front?"

"Indeed, we are, First Minister," Aegras replied, his voice as steady as could be. "We have struck many blows against the enemy, but I think that our errand here will be even more critical both in protecting this nation and retaking ours."

"Indeed. Our government fell apart that night, so any assistance that you can give will be repaid. I presume that you are here for information on where to strike next?"

"Yes."

"And I suppose that you are feeding this information to Melir and the Raiders?"

Aegras and I both winced at that. The effectiveness of our new brothers and sisters hinged upon our ability to hide in the shadows. Therefore, I wonder what good it could be if pieces of the government knew about our existence. What were the chances of someone talking too much and letting the Telurians know that we were fighting them now?

"Yes," I interjected. "I trust that such information is kept in confidence, First Minister?"

"It is. The Fiean Chancellor and First Minister are the only other officials who know that the Raiders even exist," Valiri said, matter-of-factly. "Although, due to the war, I am going to have to appoint a new First Minister since I am now discharging the duty of two offices in what is left of the Callistan Republic."

"What happened to the royal family?"

"Thrakoth killed them all in the weeks after the fall of the capital. I cannot find a single legal heir that made it out alive."

That statement had been quite hard to take and Valiri noticed the change in my demeanor.

"I tried to keep it quiet out of the fear that it would be a massive blow to the morale of our armies, but the affairs of state demand this," he said, quietly. "The people need a decisive victory to distract them from the sudden change in government, so your meetings with my agents will focus on that very topic."

"We will do all that we can, Chancellor," I said, observing two Callistan Generals as they entered the room. "It appears that the affairs of state call to you."

"Indeed. I will see you both tomorrow night."

As we bowed out, I could see the intensity of the burden that Valiri carried as more ministers entered the room. One could almost see a headache forming on the face of the Chancellor as the military and the ministers argued over budgets, debts and the supplies necessary for the war effort.

Let it be said that the work of the Chancellor in holding the nation together is needed now more than ever, but I do not think that I will ever envy him.

● ● ●

1 Lilluva, 635 C.I.

I shudder to think of what might happen following the festivities of this night, but progress has been made. Aegras and I were with Chancellors Valiri and Adello as ambassadors from the Arthani and Abuzian nations sat down for the state dinner.

Introductions were made and customs were acknowledged for each of the four nations, but the conversation that followed may have changed the course of our struggle with two simple words.

Black money.

While the Dalarians did not seem to care who won or lost this war, the Arthani and Abuzians feared that Thrakoth had severely upset the balance of power in the region. The Abuzian Matriarch and Arthani King wished to convey that they had no direct means to challenge Thrakoth on their own at the time, but that the potential downfall of the sister democracies would be unacceptable and would likely lead to the collapse of their own societies as well.

"These feelings are echoed across every political faction, although our Matriarch has stopped short of directly entering the war for fear of political retribution," the Abuzian Ambassador said quietly, just after finishing her food. "We can give you enough loans until this government deems it fit to mobilize."

"The Kingdom of Northern Arthan echoes the Confederation," the Arthani dwarf stated as he gulped down a glass of liqueur. "My King pledges his Ygdrasis to aid you, but in exchange for a pact with the Fiean Republic that may make us both richer."

"And what such pact did your King have in mind, Master Ambassador?" asked Chancellor Adello, his interest piqued.

"A twenty year lease to develop any mineral deposits that we find in your southern woodlands."

That offer forced Valiri and Adello to speak privately for a time, but what words were uttered are lost to history. Both men approached the table, but Chancellor Adello would be the one to speak with decisiveness and clarity.

"You do realize, my dear Ambassador, that under Fiean law, those riches are by right the property of the people and royalties must be paid?" he said, calm but forceful in his demeanor.

"Indeed, that is how we are going to get you your money and supply the Arthani war machine," the Arthani replied. "Our mutual troubles are too important and we are only asking to look at twenty square kilometers of your land."

"Then you have yourself a deal, my friend."

Adello and the Arthani shook hands. And in doing so, they opened this struggle to even more intrigue – but that will be saved for other days.

● ● ●

CHAPTER SIX

2 Lilluva, 635 C.I.

I dare not ask what good my brother is about to do, but I only wish him well as he is called away from Nuveia for parts unknown. Melir elected to send a messenger in the night just as Aegras and I were gaming the night away over a glass of cold Fiean beer and what few Saerans we had to spare on a cheap bet between siblings. Although he bade me a fond farewell, I fear that orders of Melir to gather intelligence may not succeed now that Aegras has been called away; his wiles would easily save the day whereas mine might not.

Nevertheless, the mission was to meet with a source known only as Buelan. According to Melir, this elf was a shadowy figure that had been turned into a Fiean Agent during the Piracy War ten years ago. No one ever knew his true name or gazed upon his face directly, but our spies knew that he could be contacted with a fish drawn at a very specific point. It was the exact tile where he had sold out his comrades all those years ago.

The lines are drawn. And now, I wait.

● ● ●

3 Lilluva, 635 C.I.

Buelan made contact early in the evening. He provided me with an encoded message and told me to meet in what is known to the locals as "The Dark Plaza." This plaza is a corner of Nuveia that supposedly headquarters black market operations for the entirety of Callista and the Fiean Republic. I arrived to an odd silence that had fallen over the area. It felt as if a thousand eyes were watching me.

I looked about the area for a long while, empty though it was, until a man in a hood appeared seemingly out of the air. And from what I could see in the early twilight, he was entirely wreathed in black as if he were a phantom out of the old folk tales.

"Hello, Helisah," Buelan said, standing like a statue in the darkness.

"How do you know my name?"

"It is not important, Raider. My spies have been watching you from the moment you entered this city. Why you have come to me?"

"We are collecting intelligence on the Telurians for more strikes behind the lines, and I was referred to you."

He was completely silent for a moment, shifting his gaze as he gathered his thoughts.

"Our chances of winning this war are effectively falling with each passing day," he remarked. "Have you ever wondered why the Abuzians and Arthani are taking so long to mobilize against Thrakoth?"

"They did promise us war loans and grants. I fail to see

what they would have to gain by being in league with the Telurians."

"Thrakoth met with the Arthani and a rival Matriarchal faction in the Abuzian government. In the case of the Arthani, the King appears to be a sympathetic puppet. As for the Abuzians, the current Matriarch knows that one false move will topple her government."

"So, they are hostages. And the Dalarians?"

"They do not care about anything except coin. It will take time to arrange the bribes and blackmail that we will need to convince them to go to war. Either that or the cracks in the line formed by your little band of patriots will save our lives."

It is good to hear that the soldiers that Fennigan and I had left behind in Tulall were still fighting without fear. I can recall their faces even to this day, for what that is worth to any secret warrior.

"Where have the resistance fighters opened the lines the most?"

"Arduth."

"Thank you. I will see you again soon."

As I turned to take my leave, Buelan reached out and grabbed my arm, stopping me in my tracks. From the look in his chocolate eyes, he had forgotten to say something.

"Rumor has it that the Telurians are designing some sort of weapon to wipe us from the earth, but it appears that they are without success," the spy said, loosening his hold on me. "My agents have seen expedition reports into the Telurian wildlands, but they do not know what they are searching for aside from an approximate location. Enemy generals speak of these weapons eventually leveling cities and laying waste to entire regions at once. Be on your guard."

"Thank you, Buelan. Stay safe."

And so, I am here awaiting a meeting with Adello and Valiri. I am quite satisfied that this assignment has borne fruit, but I fear that these nightmares will repeat themselves without end.

• • •

4 Lilluva, 635 C.I.

Chancellors Valiri and Adello were separated today due to matters of state that I was not aware of. This forced me to spend most of the day exploring Nuveia in order to assuage my inconvenience until I would be able to leave the city. Luckily, the city more than made up for my disdain at bureaucratic inefficiencies by introducing me to Fiean barbecue.

The guards had alerted me to the presence of a famous restaurant named Falisi, which was a booming establishment that they had described as the envy of Fiean society. Beers from the entirety of the known world flowed freely inside that place, accompanied by all types of meat that ended up mounted on sticks and seared in an open pit flame for all to see.

Suffice it to say, the mixture of ground chili peppers and sweet ingredients in their marinades and dry rubs was very satisfying. The chefs boasted that they were the first in the known world to master the skill of creating food that could flash through three flavors within the span of a minute. Initially, some beings believed that the restaurant was a testing ground for additives that had been created with magic, which brought discomfort to the public and attracted the attention of the Fiean authorities. After a full inquiry, the government could find no impropriety and judged that the food was safe to eat.

Of course, the entire controversy was sparked by falsehoods levied by the competition, but that was a slightly different time in Fiean society. The moneyed interests told the press what to say, and the press told the public what to believe. Falisi was saved by the tireless efforts of a small group of independent publishers that had banded to practice actual journalism, which resulted in the crowded and celebratory atmosphere that I beheld today.

As for the meetings, one could imagine my utter lack of surprise when I learned that Chancellor Adello had known of the treachery that Buelan had warned me about, whereas Chancellor Valiri felt appalled at the secrecy of these potential enemies until his Fiean counterpart described the dealings of Thrakoth in a letter. The two leaders agreed to send many of their own agents to expose the Telurian foothold in the Abuzian Confederation, as that state was not beyond saving. In contrast, the situation in Northern Arthan was far more delicate and required much more effort.

The lands of that kingdom are bordered by many competitor states, but it remained to be seen whether these smaller kingdoms were already united with the North under one banner. Western and Southern Arthan are in the process of reforming their governments in the hopes of eventually resembling Callistan society, but they also opened themselves up to political intrigue and backstabbing by both Thrakoth and their rivals. Every government in the region dreamed of union with its neighbors, but the allied chancellors feared that a Telurian puppet state would conquer and enslave, rather than allow the creation of a strong ally to the sister democracies.

The Northern Arthani had to fall through revolution rather than warfare. Until that time, Chancellor Adello pledged that the absolute monarch would feel unbearable grief. There was no other way.

• • •

5 Lilluva, 635 C.I.

Thoughts of a weapon of mass devastation haunted my dreams tonight. To my surprise, I could not bring myself to tell either my Chancellor or any other living soul, save for the mage that had known of my fears from the moment I had awoken. Aegras is quite able to confront what troubles me, just as I do when his own mind screams for answers.

Do not trouble yourself with such strange nothings, even when they come from a spy, he thought as he roasted a rabbit by the campfire.

What if he is right? What if what happened to our home was only the pawing of an overzealous puppy compared to what will happen to us in the future?

Then we will fight it when it comes to us. Until then, it is

*propaganda of the highest order. Think about what Thrakoth is
doing. He is trying to demoralize everyone we care about, and
we have not even begun this battle.*

I wish I had thought of this before I had let the terror take
hold in my mind. A terror that, for all I knew, was nothing more
than the cruel boasts of a mad tyrant, designed to frighten people
into willing slavery. They had met with success by trying these
threats on the Arthani and Abuzians, so what could be better than
to ensure total victory by doing the same to us?

● ● ●

6 Lilluva, 635 C.I.

I bid my farewells to the chancellors and left the city of
Nuveia behind today. While I will always remember the city for
barbecue, beer, and political intrigue, I yearn for my home. All of
the offerings of Nuveia have no comparison to the fellowship of
my brothers and sisters.

Not that I regret this experience. No, I will surely have to
find a way to pirate the recipes of Falisi and bring them to the
Raiders. Fennigan and the rest could use a measure of good food
in order to raise their spirits. Who knows how long they have had
to toil in the wild, hoping for a bite of a rabbit?

● ● ●

10 Lilluva, 635 C.I.

Melir immediately sent word of my report to every
deployed Raider through our chain of spies that stretched across
the continent. Word should reach the entirety of our assets within
a month, but the priority rested with those brave few that were

settled along the front. Melir agreed that deceiving Thrakoth by feinting the main thrust of the allied armies would save us tens of thousands of lives in the long run, despite the great risk of ordering several battalions through a gap where they could plausibly be enveloped and destroyed.

I dare not utter the exact methods that will be employed here, but suffice it to say that bodies are going to fall to the earth in great and terrible numbers.

● ● ●

11 Lilluva, 635 C.I.

I knew that my brothers and sisters were eclectic in their tastes for culture, but I was surprised to come across copies of some of the most erotic works of fiction that I have ever seen in the cabin library today. One would think that an organization such as this would focus on books filled with battles and assassination, rather than the preservation of such charming works as *A Time to Fly*, but Fennigan told me that Melir wished for first edition copies of any work to be preserved.

"Not even Thrakoth can contend with a book that has gone out of print," he said, eyeing my reading choice with intrigue. "Ah, *The Damned*. One of my favorites."

For the sake of my enjoyment of the novel and the safety of his mouth, he did not spoil the finer twists that I would encounter in this erotically charged thriller. It was strangely fascinating to read the first work of fiction depicting the coupling of two species. They would eventually be torn apart by the independence of Callista, but that only made the moments when they had found each other again that much more savory.

In essence, the way I sympathized with the characters somewhat depressed me. I may not be lonely as Linas was when he went off to fight and had only love letters to comfort him, but that yearning for normalcy is something I fear will never truly leave me.

• • •

12 Lilluva, 635 C.I.

Melir called me to duty today and I now ride for the front. However, my target at this moment is not Arduth. I am to meet with the freedom fighters that Fennigan and I saved in Tulall. The Raiders received word during the night that the fighters requested to meet with me and, perhaps, that it was time for a Raider to lead an army once more.

I am by no means a brilliant General that has mastered the art of leading men, elves, and dwarves, but the trust of Melir was apparently enough to push me into the saddle of command. It is possible that he thought that I would know what to do by intuition and our numerous dress rehearsals with dice, but how can that be? Real kindred are not inanimate pawns that can be thrown away at will with no consequences. At best, it would destroy the body. At worst, it would consume the mind.

That is the point, Helisah. Thrakoth and his generals are ruthless butchers, whereas you will actually care, Aegras told me from his place in the south. *And that is how you will read the battle, regardless of the outcome.*

I hope that is so, brother. I hope that is so.

• • •

18 Lilluva, 635 C.I.

I am one day away from Fort Marlen, a large refuge that has reportedly withstood the test of the Telurians multiple times in this war. This stop is merely a waypoint on my way to the Tulall freedom fighters, as those invisible few may need weapons and supplies. I know that I cannot carry much, but any sort of help I can provide may be the difference between victory and death.

The tales that come from the battlefield are ones that stink of eternal warfare, but are known only to the select few who keep secrets from the public. By contrast, the public face of this war has rapidly become one of patriotic fervor. Both sides think that they can win out, whether it be through the fight for democracy or the Grand Design of Thrakoth. That may be enough to drive the recruitment of the young and old, but I shudder to think of how long it will take until word gets out of the rot and screams of the dying on a line that has been stalled for months. Would that be enough to seal the defeat of Thrakoth or of ourselves?

So many riddles still haunt me from my ventures to fight the Telurians, yet none of these have turned into the night terrors that haunt others in the darkness. Instead of a vile haunting, my mind seems to have tasked itself with sorting out what has puzzled me. I often find that my mind has been placed in a vast library before I think of a solution to the mysteries that surround me. There is one qualm I cannot shake, no matter how hard I try.

Did my family play a role in causing this catastrophe?

• • •

19 Lilluva, 635 C.I.

I am thankful that my ride to Fort Marlen has ended without incident, even though the guardians of the fortress were alarmed by my arrival. Melir had sent a messenger to tell the Commanding General to expect my darkened hood, but, fearing sabotage, the soldiers of the fort had taken to mistrusting all outsiders. Fort Marlen had never fallen to an external foe, and it was believed that Thrakoth would put that record to the test, by any means necessary.

I am grateful that their mistrust did not turn to the threat of violence as I rode to the iron doors. So how hard could it now be to earn the help of the men and women serving here?

General Arhieu was pleasant enough as he emerged from the parapets to treat with me. At first gaze, he seemed like someone that leaked charisma. His booming voice was more than enough to confirm that assessment.

"Hello to you, messenger!" he shouted with a wave of the hand, speaking as a friend. "I am General Arhieu, and I am in charge of this fortress. What is your business here?"

"I ride on an errand that concerns only you, General," I shouted back, adjusting the reins of my horse. "I believe that you have been sent word that I seek an audience with you several days ago."

"Indeed, I have. But what are the means by which we start?"

Melir creates the strangest challenge questions that a person might ever think of, but that is what it takes to keep us safe.

"By our minds and our hearts," I answered.

"Soldiers, rest!" the General commanded with a wave of the hand. As if of one mind, every Callistan snapped into an eased position, lowering their weapons.

"Open the gate!" he ordered.

The creak of iron heralded the movement of the guard as the many locks of the gate were pulled open on the inside. After a few moments, Fort Marlen was opened to me.

• • •

CHAPTER SEVEN

20 Lilluva, 635 C.I.

General Arhieu was most hospitable to me, yet I was troubled by the notion that he assigned guards to follow me within the fort. The paranoia of this place was somewhat evident as a pair of recruits fought over questions about their patriotism, but I am glad that their bitter attitudes were not enough to turn the confrontation into a duel.

The General introduced me to a few members of his staff as we settled down to dinner. Fasti and Arduhan are far less experienced than their superior officer, yet the men have seen much in the ways of warfare. I was not surprised to learn that their fellowship extended beyond battle to drinking and fucking, for I could see the sheer hunger in the eyes of Fasti as he stole glances at me.

And I do not mind one little bit.

General Arhieu was amused by the behavior of his two executive officers, but he quickly corrected them with a glare.

"Mind your manners, men," Arhieu said, causing utter silence to fall across the room. "Our guest requires our full attention in matters of killing and nothing more."

He turned his gaze onto me.

"I know that you are an allied agent and you can be trusted, but why have you risked coming here?"

"You know of the attack plans, do you not?"

"Indeed."

"Then you know that I am the anvil to your hammer. I need a small amount of supplies to prepare for engaging the enemy."

Arhieu was bothered by my request. All he could do to express his frustrations was to rub his forehead for a spell.

"And instead of sending me a battle-hardened commander, they send a cadet who has probably commanded toy soldiers," Arhieu scoffed. "Captain Fasti, you are going to take two men and go with her."

The eyes of the Captain went wide as he heard his orders. I can imagine that he did not wish to leave the fort. Was it out of fear that this place would fall apart in his absence? I do not think I will ever know.

"Sir, who is going to lead the Second Battalion into battle?" Fasti asked.

"That is none of your concern," Arhieu rebuked him, pointing to me. "You are going to be her executive officer and make sure that the tricks she plays will not get our entire army killed. Do you understand me?"

"Yes, sir," the Captain nodded, settling back into his chair.

I could understand them wholeheartedly. The order to attack Arduth had them all seemingly balanced on the edge of a knife and they needed to minimize any uncertainties. The entrustment of Captain Fasti to my charge had an added benefit of allaying my fear that I would not be good enough for the resistance. I hope his experience will complement my aptitude for the unpredictable, that we may make it out of Arduth with our lives.

• • •

21 Lilluva, 635 C.I.

The Captain spent much of the day looking for a pair of good soldiers as I honed my skill with a blade. The wooden targets provided little means of practice other than working on the efficiency of my strikes, but I did not care. I find that I best function if tire myself out before I sleep. It keeps the nightmares at bay.

Fasti and his supporters entered the courtyard as I worked up an incredible sweat. I hewed my targets swiftly, sometimes taking two with one stroke as I maneuvered around the enclosed sparring area. The men observed me with approval.

"You have very strong technique, my lady," Fasti noted, just as I had finished. "I shall have to challenge you, sooner or later."

"Indeed," I replied, sheathing my swords. "Are these the men?"

"Gialle and Duustan, meet... a nameless one."

I never did give them one of my names. My true identity would need to remain a secret, though, for Thrakoth may be looking for me.

"Talisana. Or Tali, for short."

Gialle and Duustan are more like me than their Captain. They are as trained as can be, but are not quite as sullied by the horrors of battle. In spite of their relative lack of experience, they had achieved the rank of Soldier at Arms.

"It is good to meet you, Tali," Gialle said, offering a hand that I took for a time.

"It is good to be here, my lady," Duustan said, much more shyly than his battle brothers.

"You are going to serve under my command and travel behind enemy lines for a time," I remarked. "Can you handle this?"

Duustan and Gialle both nodded. Upon seeing my acceptance, Fasti turned to me.

"What are your orders, my lady?"

I tested them each in single combat today, for we would be departing on short notice. Duustan and Gialle did as well as I could expect of them, for they were unhardened common folk. They held their own, but I was able to overpower them and bring about their submission.

Fasti, by contrast, was much more of a threat. He fought me to a draw after nearly a quarter of an hour of fighting. By the time we had gotten sick of one another, a small crowd had formed around us and bets were exchanged. And much to the chagrin of everyone, save for my two subordinates, they lost all of their coin.

Captain Fasti is a keen man. Although I could defeat his soldiers, they did appear to be astute men who could service many purposes in my private war.

To the scoffs of the crowd, my men and I entered the castle for a dinner of chicken, grapes, and roasted carrots. Much to my surprise, the food was quite flavorful and filling. That meal was enough for the four of us to bond and understand each other, at least for now.

● ● ●

22 Lilluva, 635 C.I.

I may not know where you are, but know this: I am coming for you.

That same dark voice that had entered my thoughts as I fled from home was probing outward. Thrakoth cannot seem to locate me over vast distances, but he probably knows that I have crossed behind his lines once more. The presence of so many other attuned individuals in this world provides an elegant mask for the movements of Aegras and me, but the real question is what might happen to us if he reveals to the world that we are his targets.

Did you hear that, my sister? Aegras asked. *The Dread Lord is whining like a kitten in the night.*

What did you do?

Let us just say that a balcony did not exactly agree with a butcher, and leave it at that.

Indeed. Be safe.

It gives me a lot of hope that Aegras is still strong and fighting hard against the enemy. I felt the changes running through his mind as these months have passed. The stoic sibling I once knew had changed into a man of dry wit. It is a necessary trait to sweeten the sting of the madness of this life.

● ● ●

23 Lilluva, 635 C.I.

The allergens in this region have not been kind to Gialle today. His face, once proud and observant, had been turned into a slobbering mess of mucus as he struggled with sneezing and some shortness of breath. It made me wish that I knew what exactly caused this affliction, for if I did, I probably would have taken an alternate road away from these woods. It felt pitiful to see any man like that, so I made a sensible effort in approaching him.

"It is a problem that goes in and out depending on the day, my lady," Gialle said, wiping away tears of affliction. "You do not need to be concerned for me."

"The welfare of my charges is always my concern, Gialle," I countered, just as he waved me away. "I will give you a remedy that will prevent these attacks when we make our next camp."

It appeared that he accepted my decision and did not want to be bothered, so I simply let him be rather than risk insulting his pride. Fasti was watching me the whole time and apparently thought it best to offer his counsel as I rode at his side.

"Do not mind him," he said, as we turned our horses north. "The men get antsy when they feel that a trivial matter is being placed on a pedestal for all to see."

"Trivial matters become dangerous matters if they are left unchecked, Fasti. I learned of that wisdom a long time ago."

"Is that somewhat akin to how you are wearing the clothes

of a traveler instead of some form of armor?"

That got a bit of a chuckle out of me.

"You would enjoy that, would you not?" I shot back, grinning as he was suddenly at a loss for words. "A form-fitting outfit on me, leaving little to the imagination?"

He nodded slightly and his smile grew wide as that image entered his mind and appeared to stay there.

Oh, dear.

• • •

24 Lilluva, 635 C.I.

We came across a quartet of scouts that had been with the resistance since the engineered uprising in Tulall. They ushered us to a safe house in the open fields outside of a small town, the name of which I dare not say. The place was of little strategic importance to either side in this war apart from the usual contribution of pears and apples. This meant that the area would remain largely unspoiled by war, provided that they fulfill a weekly shipment to the Telurian Guard.

Our hosts seemed normal in every way, even as they ran their charged home in an improvised manner. They were as welcoming as could be to the men and me, even though there were very little excess supplies due to the isolated locale. As we would be gone by morning, we made do with the fruits of the forest to fill our hunger. We gave little thought to what we were eating, but some of our hosts seem to grumble at the lack of variety.

We tried to focus on conversing with our hosts for the

remainder of the evening, and they acted as if they knew us their entire lives. They all had a story to tell about why they were there and what was going on behind the lines. We listened intently for the rest of the evening until the watch began.

• • •

25 Lilluva, 635 C.I.

Shame on me. I should have realized that the conditions of this meeting were far too perfect.

It took one simple question at breakfast to realize my error. We began to discuss the day ahead as one of them, a man named Ostoth, became too inquisitive for his own good. He asked each of us about what road we were to take along the front under the guise of wishing to aid in our travel.

"Take the northeastern path and move across the field," he said, pointing out a map of the local area. "Most of the direct paths are being scouted."

"By what units?" I asked.

"We do not know. The Telurians are marching to Lellida and away from our objective."

They sipped beer as we sipped water. Ostoth was thorough in his analysis of what was occurring in the immediate vicinity, but some information was missing. It was almost as if Ostoth was speaking in code when he should have fully shared what he knew. Why would the resistance not know what units were on the march? They had spies everywhere.

"I do not know where they found you, but I am glad that you joined the resistance when it started in Harvath," I said, testing him.

"I am, too," Ostoth said. "It has been a long time coming."

I ushered Fasti to use his throwing knives, which he did with devastating effect. Our lone female acquaintance fell to the floor with a knife through her throat, setting off a chain reaction as Ostoth lunged for me. Unfortunately for him, I was able to quickly dodge and counter, throwing him to the floor with a broken arm. I managed to subdue the man, placing my boot to his neck as Gialle and Duustan quickly ran through the remaining villains with their swords.

They were bandits. Although he was the leader of the group, Ostoth sang for his life, fearing the abusive techniques that are commonly employed in his line of work. Gialle and Duustan remembered that his men eyed our equipment last night, and that is when he confessed to his attempted crime. He was going to let us go, set up an ambush along the road, and seize our supplies.

He was too dangerous a man to take mercy on, so I did not. And so, it was the appointed time for the true resistance fighters to make their presence known. This group was led by a dwarf that I recognized from the liberation of Tulall.

It took them long enough.

● ● ●

26 Lilluva, 635 C.I.

"I must apologize, my lady," the resistance leader, a dwarf named Taegan, said. "We lost contact with that outpost sometime since you had sent word. I feared the worst when I realized it would take a week to reach your messengers."

Taegan was a bit more of a portly fellow than I had expected, but that was simply the nature of the resistance that I had inadvertently created. It was a group of the young and old that had coalesced around veterans and others who had thought that their struggles were over. The dwarf had fit this profile immensely well, being that he was a warrior turned farmer.

Sadly, the struggles of advanced age demanded that he run this war from horseback, but he did so with the good graces of a female squire that completely adored him. And despite his grumbling, I could tell that he adored her in turn, even though he did not show it. The sense of longing that I had gotten from the two of them bordered on the absurd; no force would ever stop me if I found myself drawn to another.

"I have gone and made myself a fool," Taegan grumbled, attracting the attention of his squire and myself.

"Master Dwarf?" I replied as Fasti and I rode beside him, not sure what to make of it at the time.

"Oh, nothing. I was musing on how I thought I was going to leave this world before this madness began."

His squire held up a hand, inserting herself into the conversation. It was comforting to see someone so loving in the midst of such calamity, as if the embarrassment of her affection was a greater threat than Thrakoth himself.

"You will have to forgive Master Taegan," the woman said with a smile. "He tends to think aloud a lot."

"Quiet, you! I intend to die in bed riding a woman like a stallion and that is final!"

Fasti was laughing so exuberantly that it seemed like he was about to cry and I followed suit. The cheeks of the squire were burning at that image, which had been made worse as Taegan bellowed with laughter. Upon hearing these sounds, the blushing woman had suddenly flashed a lustful and evil grin at Taegan, as if she suddenly realized what she must do.

"Well, I suppose there is no better way to go, is there?"

We arrived at a new safe haven after our ride and settled in just after sunset. It appeared much more in order than the previous one, but the sudden slaughter that we had left behind had gotten the better of my men and me. Gialle and Duustan are both sleeping with a sidearm under their pillows. I presume that they will do so every night henceforth.

● ● ●

CHAPTER EIGHT

27 Lilluva, 635 C.I.

The autumn air swept in today, bringing with it memories of a time long forgotten to those few that are not fighting in this war. In another life, the changing of the seasons was a time where even the most ferocious among us would pour a mug of beer and think about what mattered to them. That which engulfs us now serves only as a reminder that bad news is to come, for winter is coming and food may not be plentiful.

In the meantime, what measures of happiness that can be found must be taken for all that they are worth. We found some of this today when we awoke to the song of laughter and moaning. By the reckoning of Fasti, the squire had finally made a move to slake her burning thirst for love. It is a feeling that I am all too familiar with and one that was made even worse by Fasti in the pantry before dinner.

"I think that we should share breakfast tomorrow," he said, picking vegetables from the shelves. "It would be most intriguing."

"Most intriguing, Fasti?" I asked, sweetly. "I flirt with you once and that is all it takes?"

"You would not have flirted with me if you did not find me undeniably charming."

I must have unconsciously nodded in that moment, for he wasted no time in smashing his lips upon mine. And, as I thought, I gave no resistance in a time of unbridled emotion. I like his company a lot more than I am supposed to as his leader. My mind betrayed my true feelings as I ran my hands through his golden brown hair, savoring the moment before we would let go.

• • •

28 Lilluva, 635 C.I.

It was surprising to learn that the enemy had barely moved a meter. According to Taegan, the Telurians are preparing a feast in response to the oncoming cold. It is supposedly a grand affair that will stretch across the entirety of the front, marking the end of the fighting season with the tradition of killing their prisoners. The only ones who would escape the wrath of the horde would be those few that Thrakoth or his Marshals would keep for themselves.

As we were seated to discuss this over a lunch of roasted duck and wine, my Captain gave us all an idea that would change our fortunes in spite of the terrible cost.

"We cannot stop the slaughter, that much is for certain," he said as he cut into his duck. "What we can do is imagine the fury that might arise if one of their own would be falsely accused as our own agent."

I wonder why I had not thought of that. I was assigned to carry out a plan designed to confuse and distract, but I never thought of nudging them into doing it to themselves.

"The fury that would follow could be enough to rip them all apart," I replied, just before a sip of alcohol. "Still, would it not lead the Telurians to project their wrath against whatever target we choose?"

"The cost of doing that is less than the soldiers we are about to risk. A garrison or two is a small price to pay for victory."

"I do not like it, but..." I said, placing a finger over the lips of Fasti as he was about to object. "...but I fear there are no easy options."

I could almost feel the gaze of Gialle and Duustan burn into me as Fasti and I locked eyes. They knew what had changed between us with great immediacy, but had said nothing of it. I would prefer it if they kept it that way.

"We march tomorrow," I continued, turning to the rest of my men. "Where shall we go?"

"What about the far north?" Duustan asked. "It is far enough away to prevent anyone from reinforcing Arduth."

It would also lead them back to sealing off the capital from us once more, but home would have to wait. I fear that my journey has gotten to the point where the daily grind to survive, rather than live, is enough for me. The knowledge that Fasti cares about me may lighten the burden, but not by a great deal.

"I agree," he said. "That strategy would be useful in getting as many of the enemy hordes away from us as possible."

"Then we shall do it," I replied, rising to kiss him on the forehead. Gialle and Duustan were stunned into silence as Fasti turned to face them.

"What?" he said, as if nothing had happened.

It was a good day. We have a means to get into the fight and my newfound relationship does not need to hide in the shadows as I do.

Either way, I win.

● ● ●

29 Lilluva, 635 C.I.

Know that none shall interfere with my grand design.

He had done it again. The Lord of the Telurians had cast his mind into the winds once more, offering up propaganda. However, none of his rants appeared to work. Aegras told me of no defections. There were no suicides to speak of. It was almost as if Thrakoth wished for us to fight even harder.

Or was it that he wished us to fight with emotion, rather than cold, brutal logic? If so, I think that he assumes too much in his quest to unite the world under one banner. For as Father taught us: emotion gives us the why, whereas reason gives us the how. Given our imperfections, it is true that some of us may accidentally mix the two, but that is almost always countered by the workings of our friends and comrades.

Except when it is not, dear sister, Aegras thought, casting from his position far to the south. *Ponder that for a moment and you shall have your answer.*

Aegras missed my point. Even though the spies of Thrakoth are likely to be everywhere, the threat of one human or elf or dwarf doing enough damage to destabilize us all comes down to a high-stakes game. One in which the perpetrators of madness are always caught out of their own hubris. For no matter who we are, we do not walk alone.

• • •

30 Lilluva, 635 C.I.

Apart from dodging a few small patrols, our gallop northward was so uneventful that Gialle and Duustan used the time to pick on their Captain. And what else could it be about other than me?

"I do not know about you, Gialle, but I feel very tense and need to relieve myself," Duustan said, mockingly.

"Why, how are you going to do that, my brother?" Gialle asked. "It is not as if you have a means to manage this affair."

"I pondered that for a moment. I could go to a brothel."

"No. Why on earth would you do that when you could be satisfied for free?"

"Yes, tell your dearest friends, Fasti. Why would I do that when I could get it for free?"

Fasti huffed in exasperation. He shot me a glance that said that he wished to be saved from this annoyance. And so, I promptly stalled my horse in front of all three of them.

"I had use for his tongue, but keep with your current demeanor and you may lose yours," I said, not realizing what I had walked into. Gialle slapped Duustan on the shoulder as they could not believe what I had said, coughing back a bit of laughter as they rode along. Meanwhile, Fasti blushed very deeply.

• • •

1 Viali, 635 C.I.

It is good that I find my life burning anew as one month turns into the next. For even as the leaves fall off of the trees and animals burrow for the frost, I find myself with something to live for. The Raiders and those that are here with me have breathed both purpose and life into my mind, which made me think of my hopes and desires for a happy future.

Gialle and Duustan took first watch as Fasti and I slept. In those moments, I dreamed of a domesticated life. There were many children running around at play as Gialle and his wife drunk Duustan and his concubine under the table, whereas Fasti and I would greet my dear brother and his conquests with love and enthusiasm. It would simply be a life where we—no, the whole world—could be at peace.

We need only to make it come to pass.

● ● ●

2 Viali, 635 C.I.

Neumadal is a day removed, beckoning us ever-forward with the hope that our actions might lead to ultimate victory. None had observed our passage over the many roads and through the woodlands, save for the birds and beasts that only cared about their own troubles. Yet, Fasti was concerned that we were being watched, so we came to rest in the midst of the Duvedian forest.

I had been taken here once, many moons ago, by a trusted friend of the family. Aegras and I enjoyed a vacation while Father and Mother concerned themselves with the business of Callista. If my memory serves me correctly, this place was designated as a national park on the orders of First Minister Sulias before the fall. To my surprise, the Telurians continued to maintain the area, as dried brush and dead trees had been removed fairly recently. It would not supply their armies with as much firewood as they would need, but perhaps the Marshals thought that a forest fire would endanger the Telurian armies.

● ● ●

3 Viali, 635 C.I.

And so our mission in the town of Neumadal begins with the purchase of paper, ink, and several quills. I had presented the idea of framing the local Captain for espionage. The forgery of documents to that effect would take time, so the four of us spent much of the day scouting the town and building up our story. What was most useful for our secrecy was an item that Fasti had bought for this very journal. He had encountered a man in the city that had dealt in a number of pieces of contraband. Among these items, Fasti discovered that the man had an interesting prize in his possession.

"Place your thumb on the jewel and the diary shall be sealed," he said, affixing a small stone to the front cover where the leather strap is held in place. "No one shall be able to retrieve the secrets found within unless you let them by your own hand."

I did as he instructed and the gem changed from light blue to crimson. In a demonstrative measure, he took the diary and tried to pull the strap off. It was sealed tighter than the tomb of a king. I could do nothing other than congratulate his handiwork with a snog, which lead to the removal of clothing and an exquisite tumble on my bed.

I feel grand.

• • •

4 Viali, 635 C.I.

Gialle and Duustan caught us in bed, but could only bring themselves to smile before we pushed them out of the room. As Fasti tied my cloak around me, we could overhear Gialle and Duustan cracking jokes and laughing softly in the hall. It seemed like they were trying to take their mind off of the awkwardness.

"I feel like I am parenting two little boys," Fasti huffed, fastening my brooch.

"Ah, yes," I pulled the tunic of my lover over his chest. "We must have traumatized the poor sods. What ever will they think?"

"I will tell them that we were having a fight and we made up. Enthusiastically."

"That is a bit too modest."

Fasti turned to open the door and was about to leave, but he had to have the last word.

"Perhaps I should just tell them about how you tied me up that second time."

I stopped him for a second, if only out of my need to control the situation for some odd, romantic reason. And so I kissed him on the ear.

"Get out there," I whispered, slapping him on the ass. He yelped in surprise as I pushed him out the door and past Gialle and Duustan, leaving him to deal with them as I shut the door.

I wonder how long it is going to take before the nicknames

emerge.

• • •

5 Viali, 635 C.I.

A few well-placed bribes were all we needed to know everything about the Telurian Captain in charge of Neumadal. The townsfolk that we spent much of the day with knew him quite well, and it took but a few silver Saerans to loosen tongues. We knew of his schedule, the rotation of guards at his residence, and the name of his lieutenants.

Gialle is crafting the final pieces of the puzzle as I write this. He needed that last bit of information to lend extra weight to our ploy. While Fasti and I are going to build up the case, Gialle and Duustan assumed the identities of Telurian counter-spies. These brave fools are going to walk right to the lieutenants and hand them a treacherous note, whereas we only had to plant a letter and a small purse full of silver.

To that end, Fasti acquired two servant outfits and a book that he subsequently hollowed out, which would make our deception that much more convincing.

• • •

6 Viali, 635 C.I.

The board is set and the pieces are moving. My love and I began our masquerade at nightfall, walking past the enemy as they looked upon us with disgust. Fasti carried a shipment of vegetables, while I carried and planted our offending articles under the guise of a maid. It appeared as if the minions of Thrakoth had not learned any humility in these past months, for their festival was joyous and seemingly without end.

At least, it was until Gialle and Duustan had their success with the lieutenants, for they showed up in force. An army was at their back and hatred was in their eyes.

"Make way!" they cried, forcing both guard and servant out of the way as they directed their soldiers to tear the residence apart. They did so forcefully, methodically searching every single room until their Captain barged into the study.

"What is the meaning of this?" he shouted, drawing a small crowd of servants and dinner guests that included myself.

"Why do you not tell us?" the taller one snapped back, ordering the bookcase to be pulled apart.

"I will have your heads for this intrusion! How dare you barge in and interrupt my contribution to this—"

The tossing of books to the floor revealed his faux treachery. The sack full of coin fell to the floor with a clatter, followed by a forgery from Gialle. Needless to say, the Lieutenant was not pleased. Not at all.

"Best regards to you, Captain," he read aloud with an accusatory glare. "Please accept this gift from our Chancellor to you. Your service has been noted and you will be safely escorted out upon the completion... of our march."

The rage of the Lieutenant had only grown as the rest of the crowd looked on in shock. He proceeded to strike the Captain across the face with the book, flooring him immediately.

"Be gone, all of you!" They acquiesced quickly and I followed them. Fasti, Gialle, and Duustan found me in the street.

There was nothing else left to do but return to our makeshift home at the inn.

● ● ●

7 Viali, 635 C.I.

The enemy hanged their Captain this morning and thus destroyed any hope of saving themselves. Reinforcements have been ordered in from the south to guard the Telurian festivities in the coming months. They will be too late to help their comrades.

I suppose that this entire experience answers the moral dilemmas posed to me in my younger days. Nothing is ever as simple as it seems. Even as I witnessed the trap door open and saw the noose finish its ghastly work, I felt that the necessity of my actions had outweighed notions of absolute morality. I had taken another life, but how many more were saved by our trickery? How many more sons and daughters would be able to go home when this is all over?

Only time can answer that question, but I think that our time is running a bit too short. We must leave and leave quickly. We begin our ride back to Taegan tomorrow.

● ● ●

PART II

RESISTANCE

Ichari nei Garde.

Liberty in Law.

- The Motto of the Fiean Republic

CHAPTER NINE

11 Viali, 635 C.I.

I had little time to write over the course of our ride southward, but dodging the legions that marched on Neumadal proved to be rather tiring, to say the least. We must have only gotten three hours of sleep each night before we would hear the thunder of boots meeting the ground and have to change encampments once more. According to Gialle, we must have drawn at least eight battalions far away from our target, but that was his best guesswork.

It turns out that he was exactly right. The dwarf had sent out numerous spies to reconnoiter the plains. The area surrounding Arduth and her immediate neighbors was emptied somewhat by our actions.

The Telurian hordes were not moving for an attack of their own. They did not pull back for a trap. They simply panicked and hustled northward to meet the phantom threat.

As soon as the news of this success reached our ears, a messenger arrived carrying news of even greater importance. The decoded words revealed that an offensive is to take place on the Fourth of Reiselda. In less than two months, we would have our answer, whether it be total victory, tragic defeat, or something in between.

In the meantime, we have work to do and plenty of it. Taegan is awaiting news from behind the lines, so we must wait another day or two to begin once again.

● ● ●

12 Viali, 635 C.I.

No word came from the spies of Taegan today, so I spent the day purging myself of woe and discomfort with Fasti. We ate and we drank, but dessert was enjoyed in the stables away from prying eyes. I cannot put into words how delightful it felt to have wanton need replaced by pure and utter joy, so I will not try.

My defeat at the hands of Gialle in a game of siege and the approaching rain did little to dampen the sheer satisfaction that I felt this day. For even in my loss, I learned a lot more about the man behind the comedic exterior. His intellect and dry wit were a joy to behold, but he also revealed that he was an artist in his own right.

As it turns out, he knows a lot about cuisine and would often make miracles with the few ingredients in a military pantry. In fact, he is credited with creating a flour-based patty that lasts far longer in the field than bread.

"It did not have much in the way of taste, but it got the attention of General Arhieu, so here I am," he said, humble as could be.

It is fascinating to realize how one small act of genius can bring so many people together. How different would my life have been if a twist of fate had somehow kept me from these good folk? Fasti may keep me sated, but Gialle and Duustan keep me sane.

• • •

13 Viali, 635 C.I.

The wait to take action grows more painful with each passing moment, especially with the utter lack of news from our scouts. These doubts and troubles were assuaged by the assurance of Taegan that these males and females were skilled enough to handle whatever might be thrown at them. I cannot help but feel panged by fears for them and for all of us. If one of them should be caught, then our doom would be at hand.

Neither Duustan, Gialle, nor Fasti could truly help me with this problem. The thought of these spies not allowing themselves to be taken alive presented too many variables. A skillful group could surround and force a surrender. Subsequent searches would deprive the spy of papers and poison. So many of my fears popped up and settled today that it may be getting to be too much.

• • •

Now that I think of it, this panic may have been the toll of getting so little sleep in the previous week. It fits with the times that I had let my worries get to me even before this war began. Each time that I had a stressful exam based upon book after book, I would sit awake for hours past what is usual, run equations through my head, and practically kick myself when I got the answer wrong. It was the end of life as I knew it then.

This is no different, but I do wonder how to stop it before it has the potential to stop me.

• • •

14 Viali, 635 C.I.

The process of exhausting myself with physical activity has worked wonders on my mind. My fears are gone once again, and I slept peacefully through to my appointed watch in the early morning.

My mind presented the strangest of dreams to me that night. I was fighting in an open field with gun and cannon bursting here and there, only it was under a banner that I did not recognize and in a land that I had not seen before. I wonder what could compel me to do such a thing. Has my mind provided some measure of clairvoyance?

I had enough time to reflect upon this today, for any issues that I may have had were resolved not a moment too soon. The first messengers have arrived bearing news of the deeds of our enemy.

• • •

15 Viali, 635 C.I.

Much to my surprise, Aegras arrived early this morning with news from the Raiders, but I would not hear it before indulging my excitement. I had not been expecting the arrival of my mad twin at all, for he had blocked me from reaching out to him for days on end.

"Can an elf not surprise his sister for once in his life?" he said, offering a hug.

"Of course you can, you daft fireball!" I shot back with a chuckle, taking his offer.

I missed his company, even though we are never truly apart even across vast distances. It is far better to have my brother here with me to share stories and joke with than to merely think through it, especially since Aegras is the only family I have left in this world.

Our fun was cut short by the need to attend to urgent business, so I brought him in to meet with Taegan and his assembly.

• • •

"I would like to defer to our friends for their views," Taegan began. "We have a thousand men waiting for our call to this campaign, but is it enough?"

A thousand civilians against a horde of professional killers—and he is wondering if it is enough. What hubris could bring him to say such things with a straight face?

"No. Absolutely not," Aegras said. "You are facing an army that will show no mercy to soldiers, let alone rebels in territory that they think belongs to them."

"Indeed."

"Our brother is right," Fasti said, careful as ever to choose his words. "We do not have the means to face them now. We need more soldiers to stand with us."

"Not to mention cannon and rifle," Gialle interjected.

A messenger came in and made his place beside Taegan. After delivering a note and a whisper, he disappeared. Taegan examined the information carefully as Gialle, Duustan, and Aegras took control of the room.

"I have a solution to our problems," the dwarf said. "The wooden forts on the border of the Blackwood. They have turned them into a slaughter house for anyone unlucky enough to be captured."

"How many are there?" I asked.

"Tabissa. Viali. Wydin."

The forts named for the three legendary hunters in Callistan folklore. I still wonder if it is a strange coincidence or a sign that something far darker is afoot.

"Only three of them?" I thought aloud, for I had little understanding of how so many condemned could be held in such a space. The forts were nowhere near as spacious as Fort Marlen or her sisters. Not that Thrakoth or his minions cared about any of that for their sport, of course.

The prisons are built underground, dear sister, Aegras thought. *And here I thought you were supposed to be the engineer in our family.*

And here I thought you were supposed to pop off. I shot back, jokingly.

Well, I would ask Captain Fasti or the squire, but they seem to be tak—

Oi! Fasti is mine!

I know. Aegras smiled widely. *I am glad that you have found some happiness in this mess.*

When I returned my attention to the meeting, I learned that my lover and I are going to have to spend some time apart. Gialle, Duustan, and Fasti assigned themselves to raid Fort

Tabissa. The spies of Taegan would focus on Fort Wydin. That left Aegras and I with Fort Viali.

In spite of my brief worry about leaving Fasti, I grew to be satisfied with the choices made. I do need more time with Aegras before he leaves me once more.

• • •

16 Viali, 635 C.I.

I may care about him, but do I respect him?

Aegras posed this question to me on the road today as we marched east, stopping only so that our horses could eat and drink. It is quite difficult to think of such things when we might not live another day, but providing a sense of surety was something that Aegras had mastered.

So, do I respect Fasti? I think so. My frenetic relationship with him has involved no harsh fights yet, nor does he suffocate me with affection or degrade me by treating me like a princess. I can actually breathe in this relationship, which allows me to savor it all the more.

I explained all of this to my dear telepath and all he could do was smile.

"You answered a question that needed to be asked before you even had the thought to ask it," he said, biting into a carrot before feeding the rest of it to his horse.

• • •

17 Viali, 635 C.I.

I had the pleasure of watching Aegras juggle rocks with his mind as we moved off the roads to make camp for the night. It was a welcome sight after a very hard gallop which took us on a brief jaunt on the eastward road before turning due southeast towards Fort Viali. Aegras told me that the mages with the Raiders taught him how to harness telekinesis from the start of his training.

"They told me that I could create unfortunate accidents or distractions, but I did not fully understand until I entered this war," he said. "These parlor tricks have saved me so many times that I have lost count."

What Aegras failed to understand was that it is not the spells that kept him alive. Rather, it was his own mind. Training can push a person so far, but that person must have a certain brilliance to turn their survival into a certainty.

"I would like to think that you had the mind to do that yourself, brother," I countered as we slowed our horses. "It is somewhat degrading to think otherwise, no?"

"Ah, yes. Point taken."

As I write, I am on watch at such a late hour with nothing but fireflies and crickets to keep me company. By my reckoning, these creatures will only be able to sing and glow for me for a mere two days more before our march ends.

Are we not lucky?

● ● ●

18 Viali, 635 C.I.

Bow before me or embrace your own destruction. It is your choice.

Times like these remind me why I am so filled with hate.

When I see Thrakoth address the known world from his throne, his thoughts merely fill me with the desire to tear away at his blackened armor and end his wretched existence.

For the longest time, I dealt with the idea that these feelings make me a horrible person. Parables and proverbs try to instill values in my people throughout the ages, but I see now that they are lies about how the world truly is. I cannot abide the existence of a genocidal tyrant with some sort of delusion of divinity. Allowing myself to be that way, to be uncompromising and unyielding shows that I have not forgotten about all of the victims of this doomed war.

I intend to kill him. Slowly.

● ● ●

19 Viali, 635 C.I.

We have come close to passing into the Blackwood, and I already feel as if the Telurians are watching us. We came to rest approximately one hour removed from the fort itself and I can already detect a twisted atmosphere. Trees are being cut down on a large scale, and I do not know for what purpose, but I can smell a hint of burning horrors in the air.

What is going on in that fort?

We move to investigate the area tomorrow, and I am preparing myself for what I might see.

If the captured were still healthy and in good spirits, then I could foresee an easy victory. That ideal was quickly replaced by the fear that we are dealing with a monstrous humanitarian crisis, for I call to mind that Taegan had described this place as a slaughter house. If we were to free the people here, I fear that months of rehabilitation would completely derail any hope of the refugees aiding the allied powers.

There are going to be no easy answers in this coming battle, but Aegras and I have to make the situation move in our favor at any cost.

• • •

20 Viali, 635 C.I.

There are caravans moving a variety of giant wooden effigies into and out of the fort. A wooden calf has been moved to the exterior of the fort and several of the Telurian servants are moving it into position. It seems that the Callistans and Fieans were not entrusted with this task, as I could clearly see that the captured were dressed in threadbare outfits.

The traffic might be easy to slip into and out of undetected, provided that we are not already being tracked. A second route of entry may be to move across to the secret entrance, yet that passage leads straight into the heart of the keep. There were no other real options, as risking capture would be foolish and inciting a struggle would cause too much collateral damage.

We must choose the least awful plan, but I am not aware of which one that is. I sincerely hope that our slumber will bring clarity for the both of us, but I will have none of it for now.

• • •

CHAPTER TEN

21 Viali, 635 C.I.

Aegras and I agreed that we shall sneak into the keep, but he has failed to return from scouting, and I am not sure of what to do. I cleaned up the encampment and did my best to conceal any trace of our presence. It would be enough to elude them for a brief while, but I fear it may be for naught if the enemy has my brother. I could not bear it if I lost him to this madness, especially now that my mental link with him has been blocked by an unknown force.

In his absence, the burden of attacking the fort falls entirely into my hands. Therefore, I took to observing the Telurians from a comfortable distance and noted that the guards changed every six hours. There were no precautions or attempts to increase security, so I think that my dear telepath either walked through the front door without a bother or willingly gave himself up.

I could not comprehend his impulsive actions. I am absolutely certain that Aegras would never betray me or the Raiders, but marching into the jaws of the enemy would be foolish. In truth, I do not know what was running through his mind when he thought that moving beyond where I could help him was a good idea, unless it was to clear the way for my safe entrance where none would be the wiser.

I hope that he is safe.

• • •

22 Viali, 635 C.I.

As I suspected, Aegras made some sort of sacrifice to draw an unusual amount of Telurians into concealed positions overlooking the front gate. The distraction was not enough to remove the four guards that still watch the secret entrance to the keep, yet the thought of having a number of Telurians move away from internal posts is most appealing to me. I still have to cloak myself in the shadows of the night before I can make my move. My hope for ending this horror grows ever stronger.

Hold on to hope, Aegras. Help is on the way.

• • •

23 Viali, 635 C.I.

After the quiet and easy disposal of the four Telurians in my way, my movements inside of the fort grew more difficult. Instead of guards, the enemy has opted to place a gauntlet of traps and mechanical oddities to ensnare any person careless enough to leap before looking.

Unfortunately for them, I am not one of those fools.

With the help of a keen eye and a lit torch taken from my newly slain enemies, I noticed every snare and monstrosity that the enemy wished to throw at me, up to the final device. It was a monstrosity that was designed to collapse the ceiling of the passageway before anyone could reach the ladder to the keep. Father once mentioned that many of these machines were in place throughout the Callistan military, but they were designed to keep the enemy locked into the fortress rather than to keep allies out. The Telurians may have had the competence to redirect the effects of the trap, yet they had unintentionally rendered it useless and allowed me to ascend into Fort Viali.

● ● ●

With few exceptions, most of the Telurians were not on alert, but their great numbers made my passage through the keep extremely difficult. To make matters worse, there were many slaves working inside the keep, which multiplied the number of eyes that might notice my passage. While some of them appeared strong and were able to survive many a lash, I shudder when I think of how I found the majority. Many of the captured looked so beaten down, distraught, and ready to give up on their lives. I watched in horror as one of my female kindred, crippled by exhaustion, struggled to heft a large hammer. She was shown no mercy.

I can still hear the cries as I write this. A full complement of the slavers descended upon her and beat her to death. No one said a word, if only out of the fear of being riddled with rounds from the guards posted on the fringes. I feel horrible for not being able to help her, but it only pushed me to find Aegras so that we could set them free.

I returned to the shadows and eluded the enemy in my push to the dungeon. I need not elaborate a great deal on the close calls in my quest to avoid detection. A slave would emerge from a bedroom and I would hide within a nook. An enemy patrol would announce their presence before they crossed my path, allowing me to perform a split jump and hold myself above them until they passed.

The door to the dungeon itself was another story entirely, for there were four that endured torment inside. I could certainly discern Aegras from the cries of pain, but I feared for his life as one of the prisoners became silent. To my discomfort, that also meant that a large number of the enemy lay within, distracted as they were by their horrific form of fun.

With knives in hand, I opened the door and caught my closest adversaries completely off their guard. Four quick slices ended their lives, but also dispelled my stealth. Four groups of two turned away from what were once their prisoners, drawing their swords. In their fury, they did not realize that the cell corridor was a choke point that only allowed two of them to effectively fight me at a time.

My speed overcame their strength as the fighting turned into a slaughter. Within moments, Aegras and I were the only ones left alive in that pit of horrors, but we would not be alone for long.

Aegras was the only person that had the strength to get my attention, for he had been lucky enough only to be beaten with a lash.

"Helisah!" he cried, calling out from the cell at the end of the corridor. "I am here!"

"I am coming!" I called out, rushing to his aid. I took an array of keys from the dead and uncuffed my brother from each segment of the dark blue chains that he was strung up by.

"You are so stupid!" I said, pulling my brother into a hug. "Why would you do that to yourself?!"

"These monsters used some sort of sleeping powder on me," Aegras replied, struggling to his feet. I helped him as best I could, but he wobbled. He had been stripped of his tunic and cloak, which had been placed on a nearby table alongside a variety of horrible instruments. In my hurry, I was lucky to have ignored the thought of what horrors were wrought with them and focused on gathering the possessions of my brother and getting him dressed.

He was able enough to accomplish the task on his own, and then took the keys and started tending to the other prisoners. They had all since either bled to death or died from the shock of their wounds.

"Help me with this, Helisah," Aegras said, softly. "We can spare some time to lay them to rest."

I freed the last of the three dead prisoners. It was a dwarf that had endured a branding and the loss of several of his fingers before his throat was slit. I still wonder who he was and what lead him to this doom. These questions were the only way that I could cope with the sheer brutality that I had seen in that hour. And so, I closed his eyes and laid him on the floor to sleep with at least some shred of dignity.

Aegras and I arose from the darkness and our rebellion

began.

• • •

24 Viali, 635 C.I.

We are still taking stock of what exactly happened in the madness that followed, but what I can say with surety is that the butchers suddenly became the butchered. It was as if a tidal wave began to sweep across the fort from the moment we emerged from the dungeon to face contingent after contingent of the enemy. Aegras acted as my shield just as I became his sword. The suffering that my brother had endured had little effect on the unimaginable power that he now wielded.

I tasked myself with a return to where the slaves still toiled and allowed my fury to reign over the hordes of Thrakoth. I weaved through the foes that approached me, and my muscles began to burn as the killing became akin to a dance. I gave little thought to shielding myself, even as I came to face a pair of rifles.

At the moment that the enemy fired, the projectiles disappeared with a crackle of blue flame. My hapless prey began to panic and struggle with putting away their rifles to face us, but two slit throats quickly ended any notion of resistance.

Whatever spell that my dear telepath expended for my protection knocked the wind out of him.

"A directional shield," Aegras muttered, wiping the sweat from his brow. "Very good for protecting siblings, you see."

"There are so many things that you have to tell me, Aegras," I huffed, sheathing my weapons.

He smiled, but such positive emotion was quickly swept

away by our turn of attention to those that had been beaten down for far too long. They lowered their tools and said nothing. I presumed that they were demoralized beyond hope, but they were waiting for one of us to say anything that could give them back some life. Aegras stepped forward to do just that.

"You are free, but your brothers and sisters are not," Aegras said, projecting his voice for all to hear. "Follow us and this will be your hour of liberation!"

The alarm bells began to toll throughout the fort, but that was not enough to stem the tide. What followed can only be described as an escalation of the brutality as we began to lead an army to confront the enemy. They were so bent on revenge that our rescue was quick and clean by any reckoning.

Our swarm began killing every living thing that dared to stand against us as we marched on the hovels where our brothers and sisters lay. While my agility made combat quick and clean, the brute force that emerged from such anguish turned the area into a bloody mess. Blood, bone, and entrails coated the walls. There was nothing left of some of the enemy soldiers after such fury was quenched.

The day was won, but one hundred humans, elves, and dwarves would never make it out of that pit of misery. I sincerely hope that the four hundred remaining will carry this task forward, if only for the ones that had shared their pain.

● ● ●

25 Viali, 635 C.I.

Our push back to the northwest met with a slight hiccup

over an incredibly emotional debate on whether or not to put Fort Viali to the torch. Ultimately, I did not give them a choice in the matter, for a bonfire of that size could spiral out of control and completely destroy the Blackwood.

"I understand your pain completely," I said to the shouting factions, silencing them. "Yet you must let your minds control you, for how long would it take Thrakoth to notice such a calamity?"

Everyone remained stone-faced and silent. They honestly did not know what their adversary was capable of.

"He will come down and destroy us all in mere heartbeats," I continued. "And I will not abide failure under any circumstances. We ride for the front."

I could not lie in an argument such as that. The things I have seen indicate that the enemy is perfectly capable of such atrocities. In addition, we are completely aware of how many battalions may be near. It is better to make our passage unnoticed until it is too late for them at the appointed hour.

My horse and Aegras waited to be led out of this pit of suffering, beckoning me to finally take up the mantle that I had earned. All four hundred and two of us began our journey back to our home and covered many kilometers before splitting into groups to rest for the night.

● ● ●

26 Viali, 635 C.I.

The sheer size of our company prevented us from venturing near the eastward road, as doing so would dramatically increase the likelihood that our passage would be spotted. Instead we opted for a much safer path across the cultivated plains, which modestly slowed our travel time. The Telurians may not find us on our movement, but I thought it best to leave our trail where the fewest eyes might be.

I am truly thankful that Aegras thoughtfully appropriated the stores of Fort Viali before we left and allocated it among our brethren. Much of it was not perishable, which made it perfect for both withstanding a siege and making sure that we could all eat our fill. These advantages were a useful aid for our movements, because none of the foodstuffs could be cooked. I did not wish for us to be seen from afar and I asked Aegras to make such wishes clear. Thankfully, the entire group complied without even so much as a grumble.

"They do not think that they can make much out of apples and salted ham to start with," Aegras said.

"That is quite true," I replied, letting my stomach get the better of me. "I will stick with chicken stuffed with all sorts of fruits and vegetables, thank you very much."

"My stomach is growling already, dear sister."

"Top it off with some pastries and you are there."

"I can imagine. Rations are a curse upon us all."

Indeed. They are fine for ensuring our continued survival, but they are no substitute for the culinary delights that we can only dream about right now.

● ● ●

27 Viali, 635 C.I.

Several of my charges began to have horrible nightmares over the course of our journey, yet word has only reached me today. Aegras told me of a support group that had coalesced around those that had felt the worst off, which allowed them all to describe what trauma had afflicted them. For some, it was a grim worry that they would wind up back in chains. For others, the loss of their homes and families was a wound that cut too deeply to shrug off.

I vowed to meet with them that day, if only to tell them what had made me into the elf I am. Aegras joined me as well, out of a sense of duty, and because he had felt the same pain.

"All I could do was let my anger become action," I said, seated on the grass. "Yet for a time, I feared that Aegras and I would die in a ditch somewhere, alone and helpless."

"How did you get over it?" a woman asked, calling out from the group.

"I refused to let that fear cripple me. In time, I grew to have many things to live for. And you will as well."

Aegras, Fasti, and my Raiders are only the start of what I am going to fight beyond hope for. There is so much more that can be done, and I will never accept merely lying down to die.

● ● ●

28 Viali, 635 C.I.

Our march continues onward with little trouble, save for a pair of enemy scouts that attempted to stalk Aegras and me through a patch of forest. We had recognized that someone was following us, but we were not able to discern a location until they had gotten the better of us.

Instead of firing their weapons, the Telurians had decided to draw daggers and engage us in close quarters combat. Aegras had fared well against his would-be assassin, roasting the male elf with a blast of flame. By contrast, I would be forced to dodge the intended blows of a killer, maneuvering expertly until a hole opened in the offense of the man as I placed him next to a large tree.

A grapple, a knee, and a slam against the tree were all it took to place the Telurian at my mercy. I ended his life quickly with a stab to the head, taking great care not to let the blood soil me as I threw the enemy aside. Word of an enemy patrol might start a panic through the ranks, and that was a prospect that I could not abide.

"Not a word of this to anyone, brother," I ordered. As we walked away from the skirmish, I felt questions beginning to invade my mind. Did they find us by sheer luck, or did Thrakoth know what we were up to?

● ● ●

29 Viali, 635 C.I.

The additional riding time of our previous night left us to be only a day removed from home. The drawback was that our charges were completely exhausted by the time we had stopped for the night. In my quest to not linger for a second longer than we had to, I ordered a double serving of our rations.

The morale of my new friends was raised in that hour, if

only because their feelings of hunger were satiated. There would be little left of our vegetables after our makeshift feast, but that was not a great concern compared to what would begin fewer than forty-eight hours from now.

At that time, our true task would begin in earnest. I had earned their loyalty for now, but I shall have to harness the wisdom of Erudan and Fennigan in order to keep it.

They must be ready for Arduth.

● ● ●

CHAPTER ELEVEN

30 Viali, 635 C.I.

Now that the threat of capture has long since passed, it feels like a great weight has been lifted from the shoulders of the entire group. What was once a people that had seemed so depressed was now a modestly sociable band that wondered what they were going to do with themselves. Thankfully, Aegras overheard many a human, elf, and dwarf remarking that they wanted revenge, which is a drive that I can harness for reasonably good ends.

As for the journey, it was as uneventful as could be, save for a spell of rain that became a torrent for mere moments before ceasing. And since nature is the strangest mistress, this pattern of precipitation happened repeatedly from mid-day to dusk. It made us feel cold and forced us to wring out our clothing, but by no means were we ever miserable over our trek today, for Aegras had thought about how our circumstances could have been much worse.

"The rain is perfectly fine, but you do not want lightning strikes," he remarked, mimicking the electricity with his hands. "I have lost more than one pursuer because the forces of nature had spooked their horse."

That may be true of the garrisons that Thrakoth had put into place, but I can imagine that the elite guard on both sides of the war put much more effort into their respective war steeds. I overheard stories from my charges of how the Telurians would sometimes fire cannons next to the horses, if only to desensitize them to the full fury of conflict and force them forward no matter the cost. My instincts tell me that such dangers will be found on the fields of Arduth, so I will need to find a way to effectively counter them.

• • •

31 Viali, 635 C.I.

It feels so good to be back in the arms of a lover after so long. Fasti, Gialle, and Duustan had returned from Fort Tabissa the day before with a full complement of five hundred brave followers. According to Duustan, the guards were actually Dalarian mercenaries and were far more receptive to coin than the barrel of a repeater. By some miracle, my Captain had convinced almost all of the Dalarians to defect, silencing what few had chosen to remain loyal to their contract with a stabbing in the night.

"It appears that these Dalarians have a conscience along with their love of money," Fasti said, following it up with a kiss. "They will be most useful for what is coming."

Indeed, the thought of having almost one hundred trained soldiers in our new army soothed my mind. Training would not be such a difficult task, save for learning how to interact and mold this army into a force that the enemy would never see coming. The merger of Callistan, Dalarian, and Fiean wisdom would provide an edge over what we would face, but such tasks would begin tomorrow. My long journey left only the thought of relaxation on my mind.

"I need to bathe," I said, brushing my hand across the modest beard of my lover. "Care to join me?"

I left and he immediately followed. We were barely able to control that sweetest of impulses, for we only fully gave into each other upon reaching my bedroom. I do not regret such actions, for we were able to savor the release all of our bottled emotions in a way that I had never experienced before.

● ● ●

1 Nauril, 635 C.I.

The temperature began to fall as training commenced. Fasti, Gialle, Duustan, and I tasked ourselves with monitoring the food that was to be eaten and deciding who would need what form of exercise. For some, the focus will be on speed and precision, which will serve them well as a member of the rangers or cavalry. Others will need to work as heavy infantry and cannon, which shall require a great deal of brute strength.

To that end, we have effectively divided ourselves up as we did with our most recent raids. I organized a group of would-be rangers for a day filled with nothing but physical exertion, for they would need to have the endurance necessary to hit the Telurian hordes and disappear as hysteria reigned. I was not truly aware of how much work was in store for me until the end of our first trek across our makeshift camp. Some of my charges began to vomit just short of our stop, requiring their compatriots to help them to the end.

The pain that had been inflicted upon them would be nothing compared to what would be truly required of them, but that is why I shall scale my expectations. After they had been beaten down for so long, the two hundred and fifty that trust in me now will need confidence to carry them forward.

I will get them there or die trying.

• • •

2 Nauril, 635 C.I.

Taegan received a shipment of Arduvai Repeaters today from General Arhieu. The elf sent his regards along with a special request. He remarked that the sister democracies are organizing themselves as fast as possible, but between our efforts lies a great risk. Thrakoth has stepped up his own game of espionage and they are doing their best to fix the problem. Even with full measures of deception, the many battalions committed to this fight will eventually be noticed as their march begins. Therefore, we must effectively render the enemy blind.

"I will look into this while you train your army," Taegan vowed. "You have enough responsibilities as it is."

"Thank you, Taegan. Leave the task of eliminating them to me," I replied with a nod of approval.

Those under me would need to taste of death in order to survive when they take the field. In truth, there is probably no better way to illustrate the nightmares that await than to ask them to kill a pair of highly trained scouts. If they cannot defeat a skilled enemy with finesse, then I shall begin to fear for us.

• • •

3 Nauril, 635 C.I.

Our drills began in earnest today as an Arduvai was distributed to every human, elf, and dwarf under me. Very few of them knew how to even use a firearm and examined the repeaters with a great deal of reverence. Luckily, it was in this moment that a small group of leaders began to distinguish themselves.

Niari, Darian, and Lothbran were of the Callistan frontier before the war found them captured by the very same group that would attack me a few weeks later. Niari and Darian were pressed into service for Thrakoth, but eventually resisted as only a human coupling could and found themselves in the slave pits. Lothbran met a similar fate a few weeks later, evading capture for such a long period because of his solitary life.

Of all of the rescued, these three had the most knowledge of how to survive. On this day, they had provided a useful lesson on the cleaning of an Arduvai to complement my military drills. The weapon had not yet become an extension of my charges, yet hints of such potential began to take shape as they laid the weapon at rest, marched with it, and moved in relative unison to each of my commands. It was a good start, but my charges require even more skill in the art of dealing death.

• • •

4 Nauril, 635 C.I.

My charges seem to have acclimated to getting physical

without much of a problem. As a test, I increased the amount of strenuous exercise today and they were more than able to meet the challenge. Almost all of them could hold their stomachs over our fifteen kilometer trek, yet that might have been because we had stopped halfway so that I could teach them how to make war with their hands.

They had no idea about how to be quick and efficient, opting instead to employ wild anger when they sparred with me. Niari was one example. When she charged me, I merely had to counter by stepping to my right side, grappling her clothing and throwing her face down into the mud.

"Get up!" I ordered, signaling a challenge to Lothbran.

The elf met my silent order and fared somewhat better. His openings were far smaller and harder to exploit, for he had enough experience and patience to look for how I was exploiting his defenses. In his attempts to outwit me, Lothbran neglected to realize the simplest truth about the coming battle against Thrakoth and his hordes:

No one is going to be fair.

I distracted him with feints and moves and began to confuse and frustrate his resolve. The tactic ended up working and his stomach opened up for a knee strike. He fell to the earth in pain, yielding the fight as he struggled to catch his breath.

"Hear me," I shouted to my charges. "Thrakoth will not be honorable or fair for your sake on the field. See to it that you thirst to destroy him for this!"

The lesson was absorbed and we were off once Lothbran

had recovered. From that moment on, I did feel a connection between Erudan, Fennigan, and myself, for the student had finally become a teacher.

● ● ●

5 Nauril, 635 C.I.

As I awoke in the arms of Fasti, I had a thought I must be rid of in order to continue on with this cold new day.

I have begun to realize why I have continually doubted my ability throughout this disaster. I had done so as a defense against the type of arrogance I feared would lead to death and ruin. For all this time, people have been showing me how to be wise and capable, yet I initially refused to believe that I ever could meet such heroic standards.

I slid back and forth between pride and uncertainty throughout this journey, but I will stop letting such emotions control me before the campaign has commenced. I know I am able to overcome these horrors now, when I think of what I once read from Luina Yunuvai:

A person can be wise and powerful at any point in their lives.

One only need look at Thrakoth himself for an example of indeterminate power could be so wrong. From atop his throne, he failed to anticipate the many that would resist and sabotage whatever grand designs he had in store for us. He failed at eliminating my family line, even though I still cannot comprehend why he would commit such an atrocity. It was as if he made the most absurd choices imaginable, even though he had information from every part of the world.

In essence, the enemy is a fool and that shall be his undoing. Enough has already been said. A long day of drills and bayonet exercises awaits me now.

• • •

6 Nauril, 635 C.I.

I cannot tell if I had a good dream or a nightmare last night.

My mind focused on creating an image of smoke and flame that seemed to last for an age. Thrakoth appeared in the midst of these flames, but I cannot tell if it meant his lasting defeat or triumph. It seemed so hazy and odd, as if both outcomes were being portrayed at once. Perhaps the remainder of my uncertainty has retreated to my sleeping mind, yet I felt no fear or panic in the dream. I was merely observing what transpired, figuring that history was in flux even as I trained hard.

My charges slept with their arms and knew what to do when in a melee, which meant that the only thing left to do was commence with marksmanship training. An extra shipment of ammunition from other resistance fighters allowed us to train without much fear of losing our effectiveness, yet we made certain to keep our guard up with regular patrols to keep the Telurians away. Aegras even ordered that the shattered targets be removed from the landscape upon completion of the day, for we wanted to keep the enemy hordes from discovering any trace of our presence.

As for those under my care, they seemed to know how to

fire their arms better than we expected. However, they are clumsy and slow to reload their weapons. The process of loading eight rounds into the breech had left the army exposed for far too long, which could allow the enemy to close in upon us without much difficulty.

There has to be some way to mitigate this weakness. I have been running through ideas tonight, yet each of them exposes some other weakness in our potential defense. The best strategy appears to be to keep our line as loose and thin as possible, as that would counter volley fire and cannon while exposing us to cavalry. I anticipate that much of the Telurian horses will be focused on the allied attack, which leaves plenty of room for us to fight without fear of being cut into pieces.

● ● ●

7 Nauril, 635 C.I.

Aegras and Taegan volunteered their time to portray the horrors of combat alongside our firearms work today. Their respective illusions and screams shook my charges somewhat, but they never truly lost control of themselves as they fired at moving and stationary targets. Their rounds have struck true less often than normal, for the faux battle with a cacophony of illusory cannons distracted many of them and threw them off balance.

A human named Aeira was the one who carried the day, hitting six of the ten targets that were set for her. Under normal circumstances, this would be a demonstration of average marksmanship. She actually increased her standing; the demonstrated horrors of combat seemed to imbue her with precision.

I will be keeping a close eye on her.

• • •

8 Nauril, 635 C.I.

Aeira came forward with an idea to solve our reloading problem, but we do not have the means to produce and modify weapons out here. The idea was quite compelling, and we had messengers at our disposal, so I opted to share her concept with Chancellors Valiri and Adello. In my opinion, the sister democracies would benefit greatly should they gather the proper funds to bring the design to fruition.

The sheer genius of this invention laid in its simplistic nature, for I could envision exactly how the firearm would operate even as she explained it to me. The tube magazine would merely be replaced with a circular firing mechanism, which would allow six rounds to be loaded at once with the help of a small circular brace.

As I pictured the device in my mind, the only fault that I could find with it was how we might store the ammunition. I spent my evening hours writing a letter to the government in Nuveia. They would be most pleased with such a marvelous find, and are likely to bury Aeira in riches when she returns home.

• • •

9 Nauril, 635 C.I.

The prospect of a competition between my charges and those of my love pushed everyone to work even harder. Our sparring became shorter and much more fluid in the early morning hours, for all seemed to grasp that they should never waste their vitality on excessive movement. In turn, the increased vigor of these students allowed for a far longer period of training.

Everyone scrambled to be at their best as we started our firing and stabbing binge even as a spell of cold drifted over the landscape. Aeira once again carried the day with eight targets in one extra round, though many of those next to her were nearly as precise.

Even now, I marvel at what has transpired. The metamorphosis from frightened victims of war to dangerous warriors had begun to take hold in them, whether through the emotional bonds forming among friends or the confidence made manifest as I led them into the day.

I wonder how Erudan and Fennigan might feel if they were able to see me now, overlooking my charges as they sleep quite soundly. It is a peace truly earned.

● ● ●

10 Nauril, 635 C.I.

Word has reached my ears of the activities of the enemy. Our agents know that the Telurians are begging for reinforcements following our relentless attacks on the front, yet help will not come until spring dawns over the continent. Instead of soldiers, the messengers delivered a host of new weapons. We do not know of their location or strength.

I was so greatly disturbed by this that I let Aegras train with my charges for the afternoon hours, for I do not like being held in the dark. Taegan and his squire could offer no easy answers as to what new horrors may be waiting for us on the front. He intercepted numerous copies of these letters from across the resistance. Some were printed and set out, others were decorated with the seal of Thrakoth himself.

The appearance of that black and white moon left no doubt about the severity of what was to come. Our enemies are going to attempt to unleash a surprise on us when we take to the field. I resolve to punish them first with a lesson their overlord will never forget.

● ● ●

CHAPTER TWELVE

11 Nauril, 635 C.I.

Between melee and drill practice, I called a meeting about what strategies we might employ for the approaching conflict. We agreed that our charges, new and old, need a final test before we can lead them to war, yet we were forced to debate how that might be done without compromising our effective strength. After all, the Telurians have numbers and reach on their side.

"Our numbers have swelled to two and a half thousand, yet we do not have a clear understanding of the activities of the enemy," Taegan said as he poured himself a cup of ale.

"That may be true, but we must do something to pressure the Telurians before our attack begins," Fasti countered, turning to me. "You know as well as I that a first strike can devastate an enemy."

No truly ideal solution came out of that meeting, for each decision lead to the possibility that we would be exposed to the full might of the armies of Thrakoth. If we struck before the main allied force was on the march, Thrakoth would have enough time to deploy his forces wherever he wished. If we did not, we would keep our ability to surprise the enemy intact.

"What of our thoughts of those behind the front?" I asked. "Surely, Captain, a campaign of outright killing would invite reprisals against the innocent."

"I second that opinion," Aegras said. "We all saw what had happened without our intervention in those forts. I quiver to think of what awaits the helpless if Thrakoth is provoked too rashly."

Every one of us briefly thought of what merciless nightmares we had seen in those pits, for even the roar of the battlefield seemed tame in comparison. Ultimately, our deliberations reached their end as we vowed to stay in the shadows for a time longer. Instead of an open hunt, I ordered that we resort to theft, sabotage, and the collection of intelligence to damage the Telurian efforts in this war while enriching our own.

It may be a more difficult path, but I am certain that it is the right one.

● ● ●

12 Nauril, 635 C.I.

In order to balance the pressing concerns of our mission with the need to train our charges, one of the five of us would be allowed to leave at any time. As this strategy is my idea, I am going to depart in two days with three of my finest pupils. Aeira, Darian, and Lothbran are going to accompany me to the town of Cuvalia, which is no more than a day to our north.

According to our spies, the town has been converted into the regional storage area for Telurian war supplies. My small group may not be enough to take every piece of food or ammunition, but a noticeable theft might ignite a series of internal conflicts and result in some executions just as the cold of winter approaches. The work of my love and my brethren at targets elsewhere would only add to the hysteria, serving the purpose of making life unbearable for the Marshal that dared to face us.

● ● ●

13 Nauril, 635 C.I.

It appears that my nights have become a study in how strange my mind can be. Instead of thinking about this war, I found myself in the realm of folklore and suddenly became friends with a vampire and a strange creature that can only be described as a humanoid cow. We happened across an army of ice monsters that grinned wickedly with razor teeth, yet fighting them off took little more than a smash from our war hammers. Each blow showered a trail of glittering ice in our wake.

Luckily, I managed to rise in time to witness a display of the wonders of nature. Several beautiful streaks of flame crossed the night sky as I emerged from our hideout, disappearing after only a moment in time. I am not quite certain about what lay in those flames, but the flickering lights were something that gave me pause to wonder about what lies beyond.

I wonder if those little lights in the sky are merely a copy of that great flame that governs our day. If that is so, then there may be other worlds out there that contain other peoples looking for a reason to hope. We could relate to each other across that immeasurable gulf of darkness, if only we could ever find a way to meet and break bread.

• • •

14 Nauril, 635 C.I.

It feels wondrous to be out in the wild once more, even though I am separated from my lover and my beloved brother. I felt at peace as we made camp outside of Cuvalia, for many streaks of flame had returned to the sky with an even greater intensity. Unlike the previous night, my three companions were awake to witness the magnificent display alongside me.

"I may not know what they are, but they are quite beautiful," Aeira said from her seat on the grass.

"You do not pay attention to the stories?" Lothbran asked, occupying himself by cleaning his daggers.

"What might those be, Lothbran?"

"The Tale of Rudrin Yvanti was a Fiean legend that dealt with a rain of fire," he said. "It is said to be a warning that there is no such thing as fate or destiny."

My dream of Thrakoth in the flames sprang to mind as he recounted the tale of the dwarf who volunteered in the armies of the enemy during our independence wars. Rudrin knew that his wife was about to give birth to their first born, and he wanted to make his home safe. The toll of combat made him so disgusted that the superstition surrounding a rain of fire forced him to run away to home, only to find that his son had barely survived his own birth. As the echoes of war lingered in his mind, his conscience demanded that he defect, for he knew that he could not live with himself as the helpless died by the thousands. And so, he was able to stop the slaughter by providing the Fieans with information that led them to freedom.

Of course, the story has never been shown to be true, but it is important because of what it represents. The fire of uncertainty eventually gave the poor dwarf a reason to live and fight for the sake of so many families, allowing him to mold a fate that was his alone.

● ● ●

15 Nauril, 635 C.I.

Cuvalia was once a paradise for lovers in days long past, but is now tainted with the scourge of the black and white moon. Our reconnoitering of the area revealed that the entire village had been turned into a veritable fortress. While there were no walls to scale, the Telurians did their best to render the town utterly impassable to intruders. There was no way that we would have been able to avoid detection in our current state, yet a healthy dose of good luck served to eliminate that danger.

The scouting parties of the enemy served a most useful purpose as dusk approached. As a male and female elf struggled to light their torches, Lothbran and I strangled them into unconsciousness. After quickly depriving the enemy of their clothing and armor, we left them under the care of Aeira and Darian.

"Make them look romantic," I directed, strapping a Telurian gauntlet to my forearm. "If they awaken and try to scream, you must kill them."

"Understood, my lady," Darian replied, kneeling over our

two prisoners. He found that the scouts were carrying skins filled to the brim with an aromatic wine, which gave him the means to create a rather convincing scene. The stage was set just as Lothbran and I advanced toward Cuvalia itself.

• • •

The enemy paid a modest amount of attention as Lothbran and I passed the banners atop each legitimate entrance into the village. In response, we swiftly adopted the composure of the enemy from the moment of entrance. The uniformity of the enemy in movement and stature made it easy for two elven-kin to hide in plain sight, yet required a rigid march with our repeaters held over our right shoulder.

The primary storage area was concentrated in what was once an extremely large inn. It was quite similar in design to the wooden cabins that the Raiders seemed to prefer, yet the presence of many windows meant that the supplies could be seen and protected from near and far. The setting of the sun had negated this advantage, for lit candles were prohibited near such dangerous materials as gunpowder and alcohol.

Our disguises failed as we entered the inn, for that subjected us to close observation by the quartermasters. The male humans claimed that they knew everyone stationed in the town and ushered the two guards in the room to attack.

It was too late for them to mount a successful defense. Lothbran quickly unsheathed his pair of daggers and silenced the guards, while I slit the throats of the quartermasters with my recently acquired sword. In doing so, we were able to keep the enemy unaware of our presence.

"We have to destroy this place," I whispered. "We have no chance of making it out with a cart full of supplies."

Lothbran nodded.

"I shall find the gunpowder and alcohol, my lady," he said, setting off to look through the inn.

He returned to me with three bottles filled with some sort of sweet-smelling liquor. He offered one to me and beckoned me to follow. When I found him, he was pouring both bottles onto the floor and soon created a trail leading to what I can only presume is the powder room. He seized a candle from the wall and held it carefully.

"The gunpowder is sealed, so we will only have moments to leave," he said, throwing the candle to the floor. The alcohol ignited and immediately spread a trail of fire across the wooden floor. As smoke began to fill the air, we made our escape and carried on with our disguise until the enemy rang the alarm bell. Smoke billowed out of the supply station, and the efforts of the enemy would not be enough, as their cache soon exploded many times over. The explosions amplified the effects of the fire by several orders of magnitude, creating a raging inferno that allowed us to disappear into the wild.

● ● ●

16 Nauril, 635 C.I.

After taking steps to elude the enemy through the day, we arrived back at camp to several reports of the aftermath we had wrought. Many within the enemy hordes had been saved that night, yet that was little comfort for the Marshals. Cuvalia had been utterly decimated. The only supplies that made it out of the bonfire were those that each Telurian carried with them. According to our spies, the food stocks would only be enough for three days with strict rationing.

With this news, I feel that Thrakoth is now in danger of losing the entire region, for a grand design means nothing if one cannot feed the army needed to fulfill it. The widespread interdiction of Telurian cargo served only to heighten the madness, for no feast would be coming for our enemies this year. In his rage, Thrakoth began to search for a number of scapegoats and found some in his supply organization. The two hapless scouts that we had encountered were also branded as traitors and have since disappeared into the wild, leaving no trace of evidence that would suggest an impending attack.

I fear that this is certain to make the impending journey of my love and my brethren all the more dangerous. The Marshals are certain to strengthen their garrisons in anticipation for a second raid, which means that Aegras now carries a portion of a perpetually increasing burden.

● ● ●

17 Nauril, 635 C.I.

The departure of my dear telepath and his companions for their own raid pushed me to somewhat amplify the training of my charges today. They had reached a greater intensity than I had ever seen before. For each exercise, movement and drill grew more precise and quick. Taegan and Fasti attributed their urgency and focus to their work with the cavalry while I was away. The urgent movement and skill of such a dangerous force lit another flame under them, for they did not lose that much focus even as they tired.

And yet, that was not my true test of the day. The valor of Lothbran is what has captured my attention since his nigh flawless work in Cuvalia. I have already tested his body, so I feel that it is time to examine the true power of his mind. Perhaps I could test him with the burden of command.

We have no models to create a strategic game, yet I was able to compensate with simple drawings of a wide variety of scenarios. In essence, I had asked Lothbran about the full extent of what he had learned, from the proper usage of certain formations to the most logical strategies used in various environments. Fasti, Gialle, and Duustan contributed as many ideas as they could muster to this exercise throughout the day, for they are on the verge of testing their own charges for signs of tactical brilliance.

As for the work of Lothbran, I think that I shall begin to examine it tomorrow. Slumber now calls to me.

● ● ●

18 Nauril, 635 C.I.

Where my charges and I failed to successfully steal supplies, Aegras had succeeded under far more heinous conditions. News of his successful seizure of two full supply carts with heightened security would only add to the nightmares of the enemy, for much of the stolen cargo was high quality uniforms and liquor that had been sent from the south out of concern over the emerging catastrophe.

The news of whispers and rumblings throughout the enemy hordes added to our feeling of success. Some of our informants on the front told us that Thrakoth is distracted by crushing some rebellious officers and had been rendered blind to what we were up to. They had attempted to insert spies into the Ministries in Nuveia, yet the perceived paranoia of the sister democracies rendered their efforts fruitless. The Marshals were reported to have completely lost their tempers as their spies seemingly vanished without a trace.

I can only assume that Buelan had something to do with it.

● ● ●

19 Nauril, 635 C.I.

It appears that I have discovered several secrets surrounding an elf of utter brilliance. Lothbran exhibited the sort of unpredictability that I had been seeking for our coming fight, yet he wanted no rank or recognition. When I met with him today, he merely asked that I steal his ideas and only make this account of who he truly was. In truth, he had sought a solitary life out of necessity, for he once was a Telurian.

His true name is Hyjir Hosgranif. In another life, he had been a political dissident who sought to overthrow Thrakoth and turn the Telurian government into a republic that would be ruled by the nobles of the nation. He quietly sought the aid of every noble family, yet his silent rebellion was crushed without warning when one of them betrayed him to Thrakoth. He narrowly escaped with his life as those who formed the backbone of his movement were slaughtered.

The deaths of the rebels did not slake the Telurian thirst for blood, for whispers abounded over what would happen next. In his rage, Thrakoth used his rebellious subjects as an excuse to wipe away all potential challenge to his rule. In the end, Thrakoth had massacred the entirety of the established order that had aided in the formation of his power. He would rule alone from then on, for his grand design was all he needed to secure the loyalty of his people.

• • •

20 Nauril, 635 C.I.

Our messengers returned from the Fiean Republic and the front with two notes in the early morning. The first brought much joy to Aeira. The master gunsmiths of sister democracies were prepared to license her idea for the hefty sum of ten thousand gold pieces and a ten percent royalty. After hastily reading through the pair of contracts, Aeira effectively guaranteed by the stroke of a quill that she would never want or need ever again.

I am truly happy for her.

The second note consisted of instructions from General Arhieu. He congratulated us on our successes and demanded that we escalate our attacks and prepare for battle. According to the letter, the Telurians will soon know of the allied plans to strike and reinforcements are expected to arrive from places unknown.

While Gialle departed early for another interdiction effort, we agreed to increase the severity of our harassment upon his return. The hour of our rising grows ever closer.

● ● ●

CHAPTER THIRTEEN

21 Nauril, 635 C.I.

The first snow of the year has finally fallen to the earth, signaling that the cold of winter has finally come, though with very little force. It had been greatly feared that the passing of the seasons would bring with it a blizzard of unimaginable power, yet what few centimeters of snow remained on the ground left little but a mixture of raised spirits and a desire for extra clothing. For a time, the world was working as it should and all was in balance. The approach of the birthday of Duustan left little time for Fasti and I to enjoy the wonders of the natural world.

I am thankful to my acquaintance amongst the smiths for the work that he has done in secret. With a payment of many silver pieces, I ordered him to craft a dagger that Duustan would find to be quite utilitarian. The smith took an unidentified alloy and crafted a series of grooves onto the weapon, not unlike those found in common kitchen knives. It was thought that this innovation would add to the destructive power of the weapon at the expense of speed, but no one knew for sure.

Either way, I hope that Duustan will like this gift when I give it to him tomorrow. We are planning to hold in his honor a small dinner filled with chicken and many other tasteful foods, yet I think that we shall savor no more than a moderate amount of liquor. While we are about to celebrate a life, we must also make certain that we shall live for many more years to come.

• • •

22 Nauril, 635 C.I.

Duustan may have been aware that we were creating a party for him, yet that did not stop us from taking solace in food and fellowship. The five of us had been through adventure and terror, so the ability to focus on the comedic tales of good friends proved to be a welcome relief. The disastrous attempt at courting a pair of female humans proved to be the highlight of the many misadventures of Gialle and Duustan, for it represented exactly how they came to be inseparable. When one is young and not quite as wise, any help is most welcome even if it is from an unexpected source.

Once we had made our toast to Duustan, we ended our dinner with gifts we had all prepared for him. Fasti and Aegras were first with the finest liquor from the Illirian Isles. Those Fiean distilleries are thought of as the most prestigious in the world, but what Fasti gave was something of far greater worth. It was a small bottle of the year 521, which was thought to be the most valuable liquor ever made. The trader selling it was not aware of what he was trading away for a few silver pieces.

"Thank you. You know that I am going to probably drink it, no?" Duustan said, drawing a laugh and a nod out of Fasti.

Duustan had reacted to my gift with a fair amount of

surprise, for he had not expected that we would put this much effort into such a celebration with the war looming. He examined it with great care as the special alloy reflected all the lights in the room. After a time, he sheathed the weapon and placed it on his belt.

"I will have use of this, Tali," Duustan said with a smile. "Thank you."

Nothing could ever prepare us for what Gialle had picked up only days prior. With a smug grin, he rummaged through a small pack and took satisfaction in letting his audience stew for a moment before revealing a book riddled with pornography. We were in fits of laughter as Gialle presented it to Duustan, allowing his dear friend to flip through each page with what can only be described as a rising enthusiasm.

"Wait a moment," Fasti said, looking upon an illustration. "That was our idea."

Duustan could only laugh and shake his head at the thought, even as the remark of my lover attracted my attention. After a final drink, Duustan thought it best to disband our gathering, for he grew weary of the long day and needed his slumber. As some of our charges cleaned the room, Fasti and I took this time to retreat to our bed and relish the rest of the evening in the arms of one another.

● ● ●

23 Nauril, 635 C.I.

We seem to be robbed of ever more time as the sun sinks ever lower in the sky. This unfortunate circumstance of nature was enough to provoke me into calling a meeting as darkness fell over the land. It had been days since the enemy has been gravely punished, so I saw that it was fit to choose our next target in that hour.

Our planning and strategy was augmented by the Dalarian defectors, for Aegras and Taegan had begun to trust in their loyalty even though it came and went with the shine of silver. The dwarf told me that these mercenaries should be put to better use than training our main forces, but I gave the suggestion very little thought until their Maesah unveiled maps of nearby towns and cities before me. After thorough study, we had every tool that we would need to press our advantage, save for one vital piece of information.

"Have you ever seen the Marshal who oversees this region?" I asked, returning my gaze to the city of Evyndein. "I need to know what we are facing."

"I have never seen him in person, but I know of his reputation," the Maesah replied, quiet as could be. "He is known as a brave human of great wit and charm, and he fights only for his Lord and his grand design."

Reason tells me that this human can only be described as a true believer in the will of the enemy, so I shall not underestimate the threat he poses when I face him. He will instill his soldiers with a fury unrivaled by any of the Telurian hordes. I must be certain to answer this danger with the speed and unpredictability that I have honed and sharpened not only in myself, but in all those who now march with me into the storm.

• • •

As our scheming continued into the night, the supplied maps were eventually defaced with notes and strategies on avoiding a siege. And for all that time, my eyes were drawn to the area surrounding Evyndein. We had no good reason to reveal the true strength of our forces at this early stage in the campaign and nothing to gain by any path other than that of secrecy. Once inside the walls, we would achieve the surprise that is required to overwhelm the enemy and liberate the city.

The one weakness in this plan is that every secret path into and out of the city is liable to be under the watchful eye of the enemy, for copies of similar maps have come into their possession. It appeared that every option would end in failure, yet we nursed our thoughts until Taegan remembered what we had not.

"What about the lake?" he asked. "The reeds will conceal you as you approach the wall and there has to be a passage there."

Taegan was correct. Some of the walled cities of Callista were recently endowed with an artificial lake that ensured an endless supply of clean water. It was thought that it would be a great risk and would add a new means of invasion into each city, but Mother once told me that the engineers built the water pipes to be no larger than her arm.

I would not be surprised if there was an actual passage into Evyndein from there. It would be most useful in preventing any attempts at sabotage and in gaining the upper hand on a besieging army. Once a door has been opened, it can be entered in both directions.

We shall find it.

• • •

24 Nauril, 635 C.I.

Our early rise from sleep to the sound of the mustering call gave new weight to what lies ahead, for no sight can compare to that of humans, elves, and dwarves rallying for war. As weapons were loaded and horses made ready, I knew from that moment on that hundreds of lives now lay in my hands. They looked to me as I passed them by and I could see the trust and hope in their eyes. Even as I write this, they feel that we are going to beat back the darkness that awaits us, even if it means that some will die in the coming days.

Aegras, Duustan, Gialle, and Fasti awaited me as I passed into the armory, fitting themselves with the final pieces of their suits of armor. No words were spoken as I began to fit myself with leather and cloth. None were needed. What loomed before us was just another stage in our fight for family, love, and friendship.

I finally understand what Melir meant all those months ago. While revenge sustained me for a time after this war began, what would I have in the end but loneliness, grief, and an empty life? It would be as if I were a shell of my former self, which is a fate that I could never accept.

Thankfully, I shall never have to give myself over to that nightmare. My love, my telepath, and my brothers were all I needed to permit myself relief and heal the wounds of the past. We are so close to seizing a happy future.

That is what gives me courage.

• • •

25 Nauril, 635 C.I.

We took great care to conceal ourselves as Evyndein came into our vision, for this was no mere settlement that had been overtaken by the hordes of the Telurian Empire. The towering stone walls and many defenses meant that any attack would require tens of thousands of soldiers to seize the city in a reasonable period of time. The Telurians left no cracks in their defense, yet the fortress possessed one weakness.

The lake that sustains Evyndein overflowed with all types of plants and grasses, providing the concealment for a small group to reach the walls. If a passage into the city is found, then the city shall fall within two days. If there is no such weak point, we shall have to leave Evyndein and search for other means to do harm.

Fasti, Aegras, and I had the duty of selecting seven from our ranks to take on this danger. As this task required swift and silent action, we thought it best that a mixture of our strongest infantry and rangers would suffice. Aeira volunteered to lead the effort, and I accepted her without question. The human had the skill to rain fire and chaos upon the enemy hordes, yet she would now be tested in a crucible where no certainty will be found. I have every confidence that she will open the gates at dawn, allowing us the means to destroy the Telurians within.

• • •

26 Nauril, 635 C.I.

I awoke to the noise of arms and distant alarm today as Aeira and her force slew their way across the ramparts of Evyndein. While we were far away, the cheers that rose from this host sent the Telurians scrambling this way and that. The enemy knew that an attack was coming, yet Aeira had divided their attention to the point where some of the garrison did not know where to rally their defense.

As the genesis of battle raged, I found a breakfast of eggs, wheat bread, and ham awaiting me at the heart of my command. As I shoveled down my meal, Fasti and Aegras quickly entered to finish the final preparations for the first wave of attack. According to the plans, they were to personally lead the cavalry and I would follow behind with my rangers, as these forces possessed the speed necessary to overrun the enemy. Gialle and Duustan would follow after with line after line of heavy infantry, seeking to secure the gates and ensure that any escaping Telurians would meet their doom.

As I set my plate aside and checked my weaponry, Aegras took the liberty of observing the field with a scope. Aeira and three of her fellows had battled their way into the rooms above the western gate. The iron barrier began to peel inward and reveal the city to all of us.

"Sound the charge!" I ordered, pointing toward the gate. "Spare no enemy!"

Be safe, Aegras, and keep Fasti under your protection. I communicated, reaching out just as the horns blared.

We will meet you in the city center.

In an instant, the cavalry departed with great speed towards Evyndein. Aegras took to the front and opened his psychokinetic shield just as a volley of fire erupted from a force of Telurians on the northwestern ramparts. The ammunition dissipated harmlessly into the shield, allowing Aegras to follow through with a directed blast that crushed stone and flesh alike. The Telurians had all but disappeared, leaving nothing for the rangers to suppress as the assault continued.

Aeira emerged from the gates above just as Aegras and Fasti crossed the threshold of the city and rained suppressing fire down upon the panicking Telurians below. Her valiant effort provided the means for the cavalry to successfully split into five groups, galloping onto the five streets that branched away from the western gate. It was in this moment that some of our cavalry began to fall as volley fire erupted from the windows of several homes, yet Aegras and Fasti could only lead them onward through the small corridors of the city.

Aeira did her best to suppress the entrenched hordes from her position above the conflict, yet her artistry would only be enough to hold them at bay as I lead the rangers from house to house in a bout of street warfare. In the chaos, I ordered Darian, Niari, and Lothbran to surround three of the occupied homes as I positioned myself with a group at the back of the fourth. Aeira and her subordinates rallied above and intensified their assault, giving us the distraction that we would need to knock down each door.

The fight was over within moments as we took the enemy by complete surprise. I was able to eliminate two with my pair of sidearms before the enemy could turn to counter us. My brethren had done likewise, issuing several blasts of rifle fire that assured the total destruction of our foes.

● ● ●

27 Nauril, 635 C.I.

The fields outside of Evyndein were once lush with green grass and little patches of wildflowers, but now the ground has been torn apart for those who have died. Fifty three of our brave five hundred were laid to rest today in the fields not far to the south and west of the city. Most of the surviving civilians of Evyndein attended to share the story of what had happened, for a great minority of the fallen had done so to save another.

Each of these stories provoked deep emotions in those who knew each dead human, elf, and dwarf best, for many had lost dear friends who had given them a reason to live for another day. Many of my rangers expressed extreme bitterness over the loss of their friends; they had blamed themselves and wished for a different fate. The ceremony brought out such a wide range of emotion and imagery that the losses began to eat at me as well. I had been stunned into silence by the many faces that had died under my care, especially as friends and lovers said their final farewells. In that moment, those who struggled to hold in their emotions finally broke down in tears.

I cannot help but think of one human who had finally expressed his pain at that time, compelling me to hold him as he cried over the grave of his love. He told the story through tears, for he had been beside her when the war had taken its toll. Niala Teituri saved a friend from the clutches of the enemy, yet a stray bullet had brought about her end just as she thought that safety had been found.

As I held the young man, I began to think about the small amount of comfort that I could find in the aftermath of the chaos. I may not have known every name or story, but I do know that their lives were not wasted.

It will have to be enough.

● ● ●

PART III

ARDUTH

Nalitu kei verna cuana kei solai unatias.
We drop the sword so that the quill shall reign.
- Alluhir Nevani, 1st First Minister of the United
Kingdom of Callista

CHAPTER FOURTEEN

28 Nauril, 635 C.I.

The liberation of Evyndein may have consumed lives, but it unshackled even more. Many of our newly freed brethren were intent on offering themselves up for military service in the name of the dead. I spent the morning negotiating the issue before a barely reconstituted city council. The Mayor and two remaining councilors expressed a deep concern for the future of their city, for the enemy had wasted much of the supplies they needed to get through the winter.

"I want to thank you for what you have done for us. Yet you must know that we are still in need of aid," the Mayor said. "I think that I speak for this council when I fear the anger of the Telurians and the forces of nature."

The dilemma of the council was quite simple. If they sent too little of their city off to war, they feared that they would starve due to a lack of provisions. If they sent too many, they feared that the Telurians would raze the city without resistance.

"I understand your concerns, Councilors," I replied. "We must ask ourselves how far we need to raise our strength if we are to prevail in the coming offensive. Master Mayor, how many able soldiers live in this city?"

"I know of two hundred, but half of these are our guards," the Mayor said.

"What if we gave each of them a number and picked eighty soldiers at random?" the first Councilor suggested. "It would be quite fair to each side of this discussion, would it not, General?"

I could only nod in agreement. It may not be an ideal solution, but this drawing would augment our strength to some extent. Therefore, I could not bring myself to be against their proposal.

"Excellent," the Mayor said. "I move that we suspend the rules and commit to a vote. All in favor?"

The three members of the council raised their hands. And so, the drawing began in the afternoon following a preparation of the numbers and a blind drawing by every able male and female for their respective cards. In the end, a slim majority of the selected were of the city guard, which would serve our efforts greatly in the days to come.

The selection and division of our conscripts left most under my direct authority, for the city guard considered themselves to be a light infantry force in all but name. Many of the guard were either veterans or the sons and daughters of that segment of Callistan society which created a militia that could be called to fight when the need was most dire. Aegras and Fasti told me that the retired would also be put to good use. The selected elders had begun to inspire and teach the young among us, allowing for the slight decentralization of authority that would be essential as we marched out of Evyndein and into the wider conflict.

• • •

29 Nauril, 635 C.I.

The day was marked with a number of victories as we crossed paths with a pair of Telurian supply convoys that had been traveling to Teitann and Evyndein. While the carts were guarded with great care, the enemy stood little chance as Aegras and I adopted the persona of invisible predators. We incited panic among the enemy escorts as each member of the horde began to disappear. The surviving Telurians seemed to not notice their doom until they met with a wall of our arms.

Each surrender was immediate and prevented any chance of further bloodshed at the cost of taking seven of the sixteen Telurian escorts prisoner. In addition to our prisoners of war, we seized over fifteen canisters of food, which was thought to be a worthy bounty even if part of the store had to be shared with our prisoners. Fasti knew that further value could be gained from the prisoners if they were treated well and interrogated. We could gain valuable information on the region just as our offensive began.

"We may even be able to turn them to our cause," my love remarked. "It may not be a likely conclusion to this issue, but we must try."

I consented to the idea without hesitation, for we needed more information about the aspirations of Thrakoth for this region. We knew little of the strategy of his Marshal and what tricks awaited us in the days to come. My deepest suspicion is that our offensive would effectively fall into a trap of some sort, whether it was through the simplicity of a feigned rout or the complexity of a new set of weapons that were being hidden from the world. The overconfidence of the enemy leads me to believe that both nightmares could be possible.

It was in the moments of the interrogation that I needed to hear the truth, yet it was also the point at which I came to see my own legend. The drivers of the Evyndein convoy recoiled in terror as Fasti and I entered their room, resorting to begging for me not to hurt them. They thought of me as a monster that would butcher them without remorse, which was nothing more than the propaganda of a madman at work. Fasti saw their deepest fears as an exploit that would serve us well. I needed to merely present myself in order for them to tell every secret they knew in the hope of being spared from my wrath.

We had expected that they would reveal only pieces of knowledge that had no bearing on what would come next, but it seems that the enemy possesses excellent communication skills down to the last supply caravan. They believed that our attacks were the work of a network of brigands that are profiteering off of the war, yet my presence had caused them to doubt the words of their masters. While our efforts had redirected many from Arduth, the threat of civilian and criminal uprisings forced the deployment of the Shock Infantry to end the violence. They are looking to intercept and thwart my efforts, yet they will find themselves trampled under the full might of the allied armies.

• • •

30 Nauril, 635 C.I.

It is our last night at peace. I dare not think of what is coming when we march tomorrow, but I hope that all those dear to me remain alive so that we can have a night like this once more. The scars of war are soothed and forgotten when I am around the people I love, even when they struggle to balance a piece of fruit on their noses to the amusement of all.

I felt so cared for and secure in those moments that I chose to reveal my true identity, for I thought that it was the last secret that I could no longer keep. Aegras soon followed in my wake and revealed his true name, but my love and my friends felt indifferent about our white lies.

"Your names are not important," Duustan said, cracking a smile. "With that said, it is better that we know you both now."

With the settlement of our final secret, I had been given the means to drop the hardened part of my personality and simply be a female elf who loves to laugh. Luckily, Gialle and Duustan were more than willing to fulfill that desire with a series of tales about their sheer luck and fortune. They deserve to have bawdy plays written about them, for their encounters with female pirates were as lewd and shocking as one could hope.

The joy of the evening eventually gave way to silence as we ended our dinner, just as we had so many times before. We were not sullen about what lies ahead of us, but I think that the serious nature of the coming battle had come down upon us all. And so, the shift in our mood had forced me to confront one truth that had been left unsaid.

I told Fasti that I loved him with all of my being.

Fasti remained silent for a time after I had said those eight words, as if he were struggling to find his voice in the matter. In reality, he always assumed that we both knew how attached we had become to one another and felt that we had an unspoken bond from the moment I began to flirt with him.

It did not take long for him to respond in kind. As I gazed upon his face, I realized that we had both been thrown into a state of frantic need. We had laid every part of our being before one another, and our emotions began to boil.

Thankfully, our minds were not made to wait for long, as Fasti silenced me with a kiss.

• • •

31 Nauril, 635 C.I.

With the cold of winter hanging over us, we assembled the entirety of our effort in the early morning hours. Every male and female who had sworn to fight by our side had scrambled this way and that as we made our final preparations of arms and cannon. Our force of three thousand has been brought to bear against the Telurian hordes and has summoned every means of courage to laugh in the face of death itself. As I set myself over them as their leader, every person who volunteered to fight knew that there was no way to escape our fate.

Luckily, every one of them had been made ready by those that I had placed in command. The Telurian Shock Infantry are marching to Arduth from the east and we are going to kill them.

The timing of our interception will then allow us to seal Arduth from behind and eliminate all that oppose us. In principle, our efforts require total speed and surprise to catch the enemy off guard. That is one skill in which we excel.

• • •

1 Reiselda, 635 C.I.

There is so little time to rest and think tonight. My dear telepath has sent several scouts ahead to monitor the progress of the enemy toward Arduth, yet it appears that the Shock Infantry have traveled further than we had hoped. I have reckoned that the only way to stop them from integrating into the main army is to double our efforts and march through the night. We may have to contend with complaints of sore bottoms and exhausted horses, but the thought of letting several Telurian regiments slip through our fingers is a danger that we cannot ignore.

In keeping with our guise of a group of brigands, our haste should give us the time we need to execute a constant series of quick attacks against the enemy hordes. I feel that it is better this way, as we shall let the fear of the unknown rule the consciousness of our enemy. Once we have dominated their minds, we shall be able to whittle down their numbers and force them to disintegrate without the risk of a direct engagement.

• • •

2 Reiselda, 635 C.I.

Our relentless gallop through the night gave way to a rapid pursuit of the enemy across the plains and woodlands. As expected of the best of the Telurian Empire, the Shock Infantry reacted to our first strike with the determination that only a group of professional killers might have. And yet, the regiment was not immune to feeling pressure from our sustained fire. From the rocks and the trees, we struck against them many times and they may have faltered, yet they did not run.

Our enemies chose to fight until we had seemingly vanished into the wild, only to emerge from the shadows repeatedly as if nothing had ever happened. The psychological strategy had begun to take effect as the Telurians fell to the earth, forcing them to leave many pieces of equipment behind as their lines disintegrated. And so, what was once an organized and battle-hardened army on the march became nothing more than a stampede. It was in that moment that I had directed Aegras to strike the killing blow.

Our cavalry bore down upon the enemy at an incredible speed as my dear telepath inflicted yet more damage through his command of fire. With a wave of his hand, Aegras cut even deeper into the enemy just as they came upon each other on the road. In time, the battle had become a one-sided slaughter as our cavalry cut and shot their way through the fleeing horde. Not a single one of them would ever make it to Arduth.

Our victory cost Thrakoth nine hundred of his finest soldiers. We were forced to sacrifice one hundred and three soldiers that we will never be able to replace and did not have time to bury. Need had driven us to the far lesser dignity of a funeral pyre for those that we had lost, sickening all who would witness with the smells of charred humans, elves, and dwarves alike.

Gialle quickly distracted me from my thoughts and feelings as the pyre was lit, for he and Duustan had discovered a strange letter that they could not explain. Luckily, Fasti, Aegras, and I were gathered to consider the mysterious phrasing.

"The wolf has captured one hundred and fifty rabbit pelts," he read. "Do you think that it might be a casualty report?"

I would suspect any sort of trickery from Thrakoth, yet I had immediately cast the thought of mundane battlefield papers from my mind. It made no sense for the enemy to hide the facts of battle under a cloak of secrecy, as it would be a number that groups on every side of this war would know. After a few moments, the realization of the true nature of the letter had come to all.

"It is a weapon," Fasti stated. "That is the only possible reason this would be in the hands of an elite guard."

The thoughts of my love fit perfectly with the rumors of Telurian activity. The Telurians must be constructing some sort of device and may have deployed it in time for the offensive. We have no choice but to carry onward to the west, but we shall be on our guard.

• • •

3 Reiselda, 635 C.I.

The quick destruction of the enemy reinforcements left extra time to rest and recuperate. I thought that the territory that we now find ourselves in would leave us open to attack, for the forests had given way to open grass and farms as we moved to the west. Luckily, what little personal contact that we had with outsiders consisted of a sale of the local farming crop, which had been preserved and stored for the winter.

We held a small feast at noon in honor of the dead, but the planning of our approach soon took precedence over the enjoyment of salted meat, jams, and cheeses. While our plans were firmly set in motion, the sheer scope of what the allied armies had thrown into this campaign dictated a cautious approach. And so, I had sent a messenger in the morning directly to General Arhieu. I had ordered her to deliver a message of goodwill to the elf and gave no information that would be of use to Thrakoth, save for the knowledge that we shall wave a dark blue banner to signal our arrival.

According to my love, the Allied Armies would be equidistant from our own position of thirty kilometers from the town of Arduth. He thinks that this positioning will create a large opening for a timed attack upon the rear of our enemies that would hopefully throw their main force into disarray. My only hope is that all of our people receive the full rest that they deserve tonight and that they have made peace with themselves.

I know that I have.

● ● ●

4 Reiselda, 635 C.I.

We awoke to the thunder of guns in the distance, commanding us to rise and immediately disassemble every scrap of material for the march. As in Evyndein, every male and female did their duty in preparation for battle with the utmost care, from filling their stomachs to preparing the horses for war. I did the same with great speed and great care, aiding my brethren just as I would lead them in such little time. After half an hour, this army had fully assembled and we began our march to war.

It took several hours to make our journey through the snow and cold, but we had occupied that time with a remembrance of what every single one of us had to live for. The songs of our world echoed against the plains as our people sang all that they knew, whether it had been from a play on the revolutionary spirit or the recollection of the gambling and sexual exploits that can be found in a tavern. No moment had passed without at least some sort of music, save for the few kilometers before Arduth had come into view.

The guns of war seemingly disappeared in those moments, yet emerged once more after several more kilometers of travel. At that time, the roar of battle left no differentiation between cannon and arms as constant fire reigned throughout the fields. We found ourselves behind the Telurian left flank and the sounds of war were augmented by the dire sights that could be seen through my scope.

Tens of thousands of men and women in organized maneuvers dominated the field, moving with speed and precision in order to counter every move that could be made. From my vantage point, I could see General Arhieu as he lorded over the battle from behind the lines, bringing a great degree of order to the chaos that had erupted around his army. Captain Arduhan rushed to him for what appeared to be new orders, yet soon turned to point out our presence to his superior. They both turned their gaze upon us and waited.

Aegras unfurled the deep blue flag and galloped across the front of our army, just as we had promised. The General greeted our signal with some satisfaction, only to be distracted by an infantry charge against their right flank. In mere moments, information began to flow to me as our eight cannons had been fully assembled and loaded. And so, the enemy had their answer as I screamed an order to fire. Our opening salvo dissuaded the enemy from forward movement, yet the Telurians responded by turning a number of their horde to face us.

The battle had been joined at last.

• • •

CHAPTER FIFTEEN

5 Reiselda, 635 C.I.

My best friends died today at two minutes past two.

Our arrangement for battle was prepared under the cover of darkness. In that time, General Arhieu dispatched Captain Arduhan and an additional number of soldiers to strengthen his right flank, for it appeared that the hordes were ready to mount an offensive against us. We observed the assembly of seven thousand Telurians in all, which evenly matched our combined strength.

The ensuing clash had resulted in the repulsion of the Telurians, for they had not anticipated that Gialle and Duustan were unstoppable against their cavalry. The growling riders attempted to frighten us with the sight and sounds of a blood crazed horde, yet were caught completely by surprise when Gialle commanded his heavy infantry to form squares. Horse and rider fell to the earth as our repeated volleys threw the enemy back, but they were not to rest for long. Their ranks were immediately replenished, and they moved against us once more with the help of infantry.

The Dalarians who fought with us had taken even more

casualties in the second attack, yet we had once again driven the enemy back. Gialle took the initiative and lead most of his brethren forward, only to repel another charge after the taking of a modest amount of ground.

I thought that my friends had overcome a significant challenge by the enemy, for they had taken on a force that significantly outnumbered them and triumphed. In reality, the repeated attacks were a mere diversion to cover the assembly of a whispered horror that the enemy was about to bring to life. Gialle and Duustan had not broken formation. I cried out just as the Telurians opened their ranks.

"Gialle! Duustan!" I screamed across the field. "Get back!"

The enemy unleashed a torrent of ammunition from their pair of emplaced weapons, cutting down a number of my brethren in a heartbeat. Duustan was among the first to fall as a bullet tore apart his throat, causing some of his subordinates to throw themselves to the earth and others to run. Gialle was lost in the chaos, which served to only intensify the slaughter. It was in these moments that the burning rage that once drove me ignited in my mind once more, turning grief into fury and hatred over the terror that had come upon us.

"Focus your fire!" I screamed, sweeping my hand at the Telurian emplacements. The roar of our eight cannons filled the air as projectiles soared and crashed into the hand-cranked monstrosities. A cry of anger arose from my brethren as I made my way to the front of the line and took the lead of the rangers.

"Come with me and take back your lives!"

Anger and need drove us onward as we rushed headlong into the field, hoping to rescue those who may yet live from being struck down. The enemy immediately moved to counter us, firing a number of volleys before Aegras managed to cut them down with fire. The disintegration of the enemy line and subsequent strikes from our cannons had opened enough holes in the enemy horde to reduce the casualties from our impending clash.

I had never seen a group of people fight with such focus, for the struggle had escalated into a fight for our lives. Aeira had killed two in the immediate aftermath of the clash, wielding her sidearm and dagger in a way that seemed like a dance. Niari and Darian joined her and covered the battlefield. The sharpshooter set to work on dragging a wounded elf away to safety, tugging with all of her might as we reformed our lines.

The march of the combined allied armies left little of the enemy hordes in our way. The destructive sounds of arms and cannon filled the air as I looked about, hoping to prevent the sacrifice of more lives to this great terror. As a cannon blast crushed a group of Fieans, I finally heard a voice that dominated the battlefield. It was a cry for help.

"Helisah!" Gialle yelped, reaching out a hand. "Please!"

I rushed to the aid of Gialle amid the roar of battle, hoping to save his life. However, the machinations of the enemy assured that his body would be utterly broken by the conflict; no surgeon or magic wielder would have been able to save him. I distracted him from gazing upon the blood and sinew that had been left in the wake of the new Telurian weapon, cradling him in my arms as his life slowly gave out. His sight was only of me, which gave him some measure of comfort in his final moments.

Gialle lacked the strength to speak. He could only muster a smile as he breathed his last.

I buried my face in the breast of my friend, spending mere moments to mourn what I have lost. The nightmarish call of the Telurians soon forced me back upon my feet. I choked back my tears and moved to lead my people, only to discover that the enemy was now in full retreat.

Fasti, Aegras, and I struggled to keep our emotions in check as a cheer arose from our victorious brethren. It seemed to us that this was no field of victory.

● ● ●

6 Reiselda, 635 C.I.

Arduth had been liberated at the cost of four and a half thousand lives. The work of the allied offensive had not yet been accomplished. General Arhieu had been ordered to press onward to guard against a full counter-offensive by Thrakoth, which would purchase enough time for additional battalions to march through what had come to be known as the Gap of Arduth. As the need of the twin republics had become dire, their General would take stock of the battle in the early morning before marching off to war once more.

His first act was appointing my dear brother as the interim military governor, which was little more than a formality, as the true appointee was mere days away. He reasoned that the town would need someone to account for the tasks that the bureaucrats would not wish to handle. Their task would be to oversee the military occupation in the name of the Chancellor. It was hoped that they would be able to fully reconstitute the regional civilian government, but the military could make no guarantee to that end.

"You have taken no oath to serve, so you are both free to leave once the governor arrives," Arhieu said. "Captain Fasti and your militia will ride with me to the east."

The losses of my brethren had been incredibly high, but the thought of earning some money and continuing to destroy the Telurian hordes had proven to be too tempting for them to ignore. I held to thoughts of hope for them, for they were to be placed under the command of Fasti for the duration of the offensive. The care of my love would allow them to survive the war and rebuild their lives, which was what truly mattered in the end.

The General and his subordinates had given us mere moments to say our final farewells, if only to ensure that our parting would not shatter our lives. I can only assume that he knew that our relationship had blossomed from our relaxed demeanor toward one another, which had been so different from the time that we met.

Fasti emerged from the quarters of General Arhieu as a Captain once more, wasting little time in directing Aeira, Niari, and Darian to assemble his command staff for the march to war. In spite of the activity around him, the sole focus of Fasti was on Aegras and me.

"You will be missed, my brother," Fasti said, pulling

Aegras into a hug.

"You will be as well," my brother replied, smiling as he clasped the shoulder of my lover.

Fasti released my dear telepath from his grasp and turned to me. For a time, we could do nothing but gaze upon one another in silence. It seemed that all of our memories passed before us. The time that we had first laid eyes upon one another quickly gave way to all of the laughter and joy that we had felt in the company of one another.

"How could I say farewell to the one I love?" Fasti wondered, looking upon me with a ferocious intensity.

"You are coming back to me," I said with a smile. "That is all I could ever accept."

He pulled me into one last kiss, pouring all of his feelings into the moment as he had done over the long months. In turn, I gave him all of mine.

"Until we meet again, Helisah."

"Until we meet again, Fasti."

He turned away and returned to his horse, swiftly mounting the animal. In a moment, he and all of the others had left Aegras and me alone, allowing me to release that one tear of joy.

I know that this is not our end.

• • •

7 Reiselda, 635 C.I.

Many battalions marched through Arduth on their path to join the war today. I tasked myself with deciphering the mysteries of the retreating enemy. The Telurians had left behind a mountain of documents and statistics, failing to burn their most secret information as they fled the town before us. I was directed to their former headquarters at the Red Lady Tavern, which was in the process of being ransacked by Callistan and Fiean agents when I arrived. They had gathered every paper that they could find over the long hours of the night.

The Telurians had guessed that an attack was coming, but they had utterly fallen for the thought that we were going to take back Agosia by the dawn of spring. The commanding Marshals had focused their attention elsewhere in the weeks leading up to our attack, for they had been given false information that tens of thousands of soldiers were amassing for a landing from the northern seas. The appearance of our previous deceptions and those of the Raiders had also served this narrative, for they had focused upon assessing our strength and found nothing to be of use. These failures swiftly lead to silence from their spies for one reason or another.

I took a rest in order to meet with Aegras for our meal, learning of how my dear telepath has taken to his temporary role. He reminded me of a junior statesman as he discussed construction and defensive efforts with a group of military engineers, setting them to work on the projects that would least offend the approaching governor. The meeting lasted for fifteen minutes, leaving me with an intense hunger by the time that Aegras was aware of my presence.

After a brief while, we settled in for a modest feast of

vegetable stew, bread, and water, which had become a luxury for the occupied territories as winter took hold. Under normal circumstances, the people always stored enough to eat their fill in the cold. The presence of a hostile army had utterly destroyed their ability to feed themselves. Aegras thought that this was due in part to the complete disruption of the flow of free enterprise between the sister democracies, which would need to be reconstituted as spring approaches.

"General Arhieu sent a message to the chancellors before he marched," Aegras said. "The town is almost depleted of the barest of necessities."

"I assume that the Fiean Government will act?" I asked, sipping the heated broth.

"Yes, but it will take time. I fear that they do not have many days left to save this place."

Our immediate concerns were set aside as a Callistan agent known as Farran burst into the room. The elf had a demeanor that was filled with worry, which was made apparent as he readied the two papers that had been found in a bedroom in the Red Lady. Farran strode to Aegras and me in great haste, speaking with an undercurrent of panic as he gave Aegras a letter and a diagram.

The Telurians are constructing an explosive device beyond the range of any existing technology. According to the letter and engineering specifications, the device appears to harness a previously unknown energy source that counters the essence of magic, creating a force that turns humans, elves, and dwarves to dust. I shudder at the thought of how Thrakoth came to discover this new nightmare, for I cannot fathom that anyone would willingly give themselves up to such a torturous doom. The disappearance and death of those who dared to resist and those too weak to carry on would be far too useful for Thrakoth to ignore, whether it was to further the horrors that he might unleash upon the world or to remind others of his domination.

There is still time to counter the scientists of the Telurian Empire, for they have not constructed a working device. My first chance at making sure that they are never able to build this threat will come about with the capture of the engineer who wrote these pieces. Luckily, the mad elf supplied his name and the location of his central laboratory in the city of Tarilonis.

We shall ride to the east and burn their prize.

• • •

8 Reiselda, 635 C.I.

The arrival of the new governor gave us permission to unleash our wrath upon the Telurians once more. The new human governor took over quite swiftly after my brother informed her of the administrative issues in Arduth. The recovery will take an incredible amount of time to accomplish, largely due in part to the expectation of snow and rationing in the near future. The Fieans were expected to arrive with aid in the coming days, yet worries began to arise over how the town might survive.

She had volunteered for this incredible burden on the recommendation of other civil servants, for she saw the recovery of Callista as a symbol of hope for the future. With a great amount of skill and some luck, the news of victory and healing will spread like flame to those who live on. Chancellor Valiri expressed thoughts about how the news of a national rebirth would encourage the army to fight harder, yet might also convince Dalarians and Abuzians to enter the war.

Aegras made certain to dispatch news of the Telurian weapons program to the chancellors in Nuveia, for they would need to prepare for every scenario imaginable. It is probable that these tricks of the enemy might appear in battles to come, so we assumed that the collection of information would be a necessary and proper course of action in addition to the arts of killing and sabotage. If we should be successful, we will prevent the Telurians from ever engineering such horrible weapons again. Realistically, we may only be able to delay their efforts for a few months, which would buy us the time to move elsewhere with great urgency.

In spite of the new dangers that await, I managed to find a little bit of happiness with the arrival of a package from Melir. It consisted of a letter and some food that had been prepared for Aegras and me, which demonstrated how the love of a family can never truly die. The salted venison would be useful in the coming days, especially since the conditions in the wild do not favor the preparation and enjoyment of a hearty meal.

The smell of the prepared meat brought back memories of those days where I had no task but to learn, grow, and fight for my present stature as a free elf. Melir and his Raiders gave us so much in these times, yet the offering of a small piece of home made me shed a tear of joy. While this feeling may have been brief, I think that I shall always be reminded of it, for the final words of the letter have been burned into my mind just as they shall be immortalized here.

The two of you are loved and the entire world rides with you.

• • •

CHAPTER SIXTEEN

10 Reiselda, 635 C.I.

Nothing of note had happened yesterday, leaving me with little desire to write of the mundane details of my life. Aegras and I simply pressed onward with the wind at our backs, enjoying the peace that could be found as we galloped across the frigid land.

We found some luck today: we crossed paths with a wild boar, which had been feasting upon the roots of a plant when we came upon it. The animal immediately turned to charge at us, yet Aegras proved to be more than a match, as he raised the animal into the air. The exercise of such an immense power allowed me to approach the boar and slit its throat without incident. Our excellent example of teamwork allowed us to eat quite well on this night, even though so much pain had to be taken to carve up, cook, and prepare the remaining meat for our journey.

I wish that my dear telepath had a spell that could help with such matters.

We spent three hours on the open field. In that time, we had been concerned with the presentation of new threats in the form of uneven snow, chilling wind, and the thought that our fire would attract unwanted attention. Luckily, Aegras was able to subdue the smoke with a strange powder that he had recently acquired. As he threw the dust into the fire, the smoke changed color from dark gray to white, allowing it to blend with the clouds above us in an inconspicuous manner. Our fear of discovery by the rear guard of our enemy had been met with the song of the birds and little else, for not a single male or female could be seen in the desolate winter.

• • •

There is nothing in this grand undertaking that shall resist my will.

Thrakoth cast his thoughts into the wind once more after a long absence, interrupting my attempt at slumber with new images of death and devastation. The screams of the doomed filled our minds as our vision was overtaken by a blue light. It was here that we witnessed a human female struggling against her shackles, only to be roasted into ash by the machine that had been placed in her small tomb.

The cruelty that the Telurian Empire had employed would be forever elevated by this glimpse into the mind of their Lord. These new tortures only incited a burning hatred within my twin and me that we had never felt before. I can feel the entirety of our collective anger and restlessness as the night drags onward. The images that had been burned into our minds will ensure that we will not sleep well on this night.

I hope that our rage can be put to rest when we reach Tarilonis, but I think that it shall not be so.

• • •

13 Reiselda, 635 C.I.

The continent is becoming more of a desolate wasteland as we make our way to the east, for even the singing of the birds has passed away. The wild has become quite devoid of life in these past months, especially with the arrival of a winter storm in the early morning hours. The cold made certain that very few of those who lived in solitude would survive, especially with the continued demands of the enemy upon the captive populace. Luckily, Aegras and I have yet to be accosted by any sentient creatures as we make for Tarilonis.

We have been struggling to keep warm as waves of snow sweep across the land, yet the problem was solved with time and no small amount of effort. We have found some protection from the weather by taking shelter in abandoned farms and cabins, which did little to stave off the temperature but gave us a strong shield against the wind and precipitation. I suspect that we shall find little comfort even in these apparent fortresses, for they only serve as a reminder of how fragile our lives can truly be.

I am trying to forget what I saw in the previous encampment, which served only as a reminder of the darkness that can loom over us all. It wounds me when I observe what might happen when people completely and utterly lose hope, and the horror of the previous night had been no exception.

We came across a human family that had been utterly decimated by the thieves and murderers that have awoken in the midst of war. The mother and her four children lay in the barn, murdered by a monstrous being that had seen it fit to bind and decapitate them. We found the father mere meters away with a bullet in his head and a sidearm in hand. The atrocity had been preserved by the cold, which had given little quarter to the wild animals or insects that might desecrate their bodies. Aegras wondered if we should bury the dead with some form of dignity, but we sought respite from the horrors that we saw by taking shelter in the residence.

I want to forget that grisly deed. I want to cast it out of my mind and think no more of it, yet I think that I will never do so. I can only remind myself of the lessons that I have learned about our nature. Imperfections and dark deeds shall always be in the world, but I do not believe that these will ever go unchallenged. The darkness of the world will be countered by the actions of an ordinary person, for every human, elf, and dwarf is capable of extraordinary feats of courage and strength even when doubt and danger can get the better of them. The deeds of those people will be what restores this world to life, preparing the way for a time when justice and relief can be given to our six kindred and the many that have suffered through the fire.

However, that time is not at hand.

● ● ●

15 Reiselda, 635 C.I.

I am grateful that Aegras is with me on this ride, for he has helped me find solace in the incessant cold. The addition of a few games that we had found in another abandoned residence provided a good means to pass the time. We had not been able to play many of these old favorites on a regular basis for five years or more. There was simply too much to do in our days of formal schooling; the desire to go to the Royal College met with a curriculum that intensified with each passing year. Aegras and I had to move between history, art, mathematics, and politics with the grace that we now command our arms and minds.

I reveled in the intense and concentrated effort that we had both placed upon capturing pieces and moving around the board. We would always find a means to beat one another after a battle of wits and strategy, which had exercised our mind tonight just as it had done many years prior. Neither of us would ever exploit our connection as a means to achieve victory, as our Mother had provided an explanation that had been quite convincing. She had said that fairness is required in the world of gaming just as it was in life itself. To this day, I wonder if that lesson was ever meant to be applied to my adult life, especially since I have learned of her true nature as a spy.

I may be cold on this night, but I am quite grateful that my nature is very much intact despite all that has happened.

• • •

16 Reiselda, 635 C.I.

A farmer and his wife have granted us shelter tonight in the midst of a gust of wind that carries snow across the land even at this moment. Our initial attempt to convince the male elf and his pregnant bride of our intentions was not easy in the least. They assumed that any passing life would be brigands or Telurian scouts. Thankfully, we were able to talk our way into their company with the offer of a trade of ammunition for food. We had enough in the way of arms for the fight to come and they had an abundance of food, so peace rather than violence ruled the day.

We ate in the comfort of a heated home for the first time in a week, a welcome relief from the very real danger of succumbing to the wrath of nature. We could not fully rest until later at night due to the need to alleviate the suspicions of our hosts. Tamrin had his eye upon us for the entirety of the dinner as we ate roasted pheasant and drank water. As a contingency, my dear telepath had done his duty and quietly activated the safety locks on the weapon with his mind, granting us precious seconds to disarm them if they wished us harm.

They had not done so.

Aegras and I can appreciate the desire of Tamrin to protect Asywin and their child from harm, but we sternly relayed our friendly intentions to them by stating obvious truths. They were fellow Callistans under the same dilemma as so many others in this war, and fear got the better of them until we demonstrated how far the war had turned in our favor. With some tact and grace, we got them to lower their weapons and treat us as acquaintances instead of potential enemies. After a time, their fear of the unknown turned into a small expression of hospitality as they supplied some spare blankets for the night, but that was all that they could give to wanderers like us.

● ● ●

17 Reiselda, 635 C.I.

I find myself in a better mood today, for the wind and snow has ceased and the sun has emerged once more. The illumination and warmth of our mother star would not be enough to melt the snow or eliminate the need for our coats, but it allowed us to press on without the fear of any sort of tribulation. With a small payment of silver to Tamrin for his hospitality, we were able to ride to the east across fields filled with snow. Aegras and I felt no discomfort as our steeds proved to be adept at navigating through the terrain.

I began to mumble the words of many songs that I have learned from traveling musicians and my own soldiers, yet I keep coming back to the ideals expressed when a human wrote a ballad called "One Wounded Heart." The song was supposedly written to honor one of the first healers of Callista, but most of the sayings in the song were expressed by many of those that would become our legends. It had been used since those days out of the thought that we might finally grow out of our feuds and struggles and allow those that follow to live and study in a world of peace and abundance.

At the very least, that is what I was told. The truth had to have been somewhat muddled as the tale grew and time passed, but I think that the ideals are noble and may come to be within our grasp as time passes. We will grow progressively more intelligent and press on in our quest to be better than before, but it has to be done with all of the disagreements and trouble that comes with life and liberty rather than through the cold kiss of a metal cage.

I think that we are nearing the end of our journey in a few days, for we have come across signs of life. Nature has seen fit to preserve a certain amount of footprints and cart wheels that lead to an old junction along the roads. The wood has warped with the passage of time, yet the measurements were clearly displayed for all who passed. Tarilonis is several hundred kilometers to our east, and our worries shall intensify in the coming days until we pass into the shadows once more. It is my hope that the Telurians can aid us with a certain measure of cooperation.

● ● ●

19 Reiselda, 635 C.I.

Aegras is quite pleased with the progress that we have made in these past days, but I am quite wary of what we might find at the end of this particular journey. With all of the horrible events to which I have borne witness in this war, the question of what lies ahead arose in my mind as I lay by the fire. I am not sure if I know how to deal with the possible relationship between the horror of these secret weapons and the ideals of a grand design that I now see scrawled across residences and businesses. Is it possible that these weapons are a symptom of the madness of a tyrant or the discovery that compelled Thrakoth to action?

These answers are equally terrifying in what they imply for the future of the world. It is entirely possible that these weapons will be a means to nullify the recent victories of the sister democracies, but I think that the most potent danger is that a common fear of the unknown might drive the world into madness. We do not know what these experiments are capable of unleashing upon the world. That uncertainty may compel all those who stand against the enemy to react in unexpected and potentially dangerous ways. I may be young in the eyes of the world, but I do know that every being is beholden to a combination of reason and emotion. That simple truth makes it hard to predict whether a piece of the old world may stand after this conflict has concluded.

● ● ●

21 Reiselda, 635 C.I.

The city of Tarilonis now stretches out across a large expanse of the land on two banks of the Nelduhan River. It had been quite easy to gain passage into the city due to a wide variety of entrances that were guarded by conscripted militia. The city was defended by two forts that overlooked either side of the river, but they appear to be designed to protect the city from a full scale assault from land and sea. The Telurian hordes had done their best to restore the forts to full strength and now use the twin installations to quarter many of their elite soldiers.

I anticipate that we will remain secret as long as we can keep ourselves sheltered in the center of Tarilonis, for we were not accosted after entering the city from the south and west. In truth, the city and her residents appear to have approached a normalcy resembling the years before the conflict. There was some damage in places from the firing of arms, but much of it was either ignored or quickly repaired by the artisans that had remained in the city. It was quite strange to see a normal way of life in the midst of such chaos, but Aegras quickly thought of why this might be the case.

"It is quite possible that the Telurian Marshal has a

different philosophy than what we have seen," he said, just as we sat down for a private meal. "If you create an illusion that every aspect of a life can be normal and prosperous again, would your subjects not simply enjoy their lives and fail to question any mysterious happenings?"

My dear brother provided a grand argument, but I had to disagree because of what had been missing from our discussion.

"You neglect the idea of ruling through fear, Aegras," I countered. "Those who dare to inquire about a strange deed or two are liable to be silenced, so there is no incentive to do so because of the preservation of the self."

Neither of us conceded the argument, but I think that it is because both of us were right in some small way. Our discussion provided some form of insight into why the Telurians would hide the research of such destructive weapons under the guise of a recovered city. The usage of violence is not necessarily the most dangerous concept that has ever been shone upon a being. It is the idea of living under the inescapable threat of violence that can make a human, elf, or dwarf easy to control, even if they might not think that such matters of the mind are really affecting them.

I suppose that my brother and I will be able to understand the scope and scale of this madness in the coming days, for there is much to do if we are to find out where the enemy secretly lurks.

● ● ●

CHAPTER SEVENTEEN

22 Reiselda, 635 C.I.

Aegras and I began to observe the movements of the enemy within Tarilonis today. Unfortunately, each portion of the occupying force is far more decentralized than we have previously seen. The scientists and soldiers do not contain themselves within separated castes, and they possess a great appreciation for secrecy. We have not heard them speak of their work in public, though they have considered details of their sexual exploits with willing Callistan females to be a more worthy topic of discussion.

In spite of the lack of loosened tongues, Aegras may have found a potential target in the form of a female elf. Whereas the rest of the enemy appeared to be in a celebratory mood, my dear telepath described the unnamed Telurian as one under much duress. The language of the body appeared to tell much of the tale to my brother as he investigated from afar, but her silence was the most telling sign of a being that had been damaged.

It appears that her mind is in crisis, Aegras thought. *I shall observe her for the rest of the evening and see if there is any truth to my suspicions.*

Aegras may not have returned to our current hiding place

in The Rose and Carrot Tavern, but he has taken care to avoid any questionable situations as the night wears on. He is merely observing this elf from the shadows in an attempt to understand what troubles her. If her disturbance is inconsequential, then we will simply find another way. I remain hopeful that this mysterious elf will be of use to us in the near future.

• • •

23 Reiselda, 635 C.I.

Aegras returned with some news of his target as I awoke in the late morning. I suppose that what he encountered should have been an expected part of travel within the lands now controlled by Thrakoth. After a time, the elf departed from her group and attempted to evade any being that might be watching. Once she had been convinced of her anonymity, she found an alley and produced a piece of chalk from her pocket. At his vantage point above the alley, Aegras could see she had drawn a small star in an easily missed position.

We had stumbled across what we had thought to be the work of Fiean Intelligence. Since we did not wish to hinder the war effort, we spent a great deal of time guarding ourselves against all of the ways that our interference might end in disaster. Aegras thought that we should observe the meeting in order to protect the agent and the source, for it stands to reason that one or both of the participants might be lying about what was about to happen. It is quite possible that the signaling of the agent might actually be an elaborately constructed trap to lure suspected traitors or spies to their doom.

Unfortunately, we have no way of understanding this matter until the meeting begins.

● ● ●

24 Reiselda, 635 C.I.

Our continued observation of the Telurian revealed that her intentions were pure and motivated by personal doubts, but we found no traces of mysterious visitors to the city. These occurrences led us to believe that the recruiter of our unnamed subject had been placed where the enemy would not see him or her. Aegras suggested that he might be a respected member of the local community that was biding his time and feeding information back to the allied powers. Unfortunately, the forces of gossip and bribery did very little to aid in our determination of this matter.

We are on our own.

My brother and I keep watch over our subject even now, for she seems to be the only way to move forward with our plot of sabotage. In spite of her assumed riches as a trusted scientist in the Telurian fold, our subject exhibits all of the characteristics of a very simple life, from the selection of her clothing to her choice of company. It is quite possible that this elf may have access to highly secretive Telurian research, but may not have known what was occurring in this city until she had found the horrors that Thrakoth wished upon the world. That form of decentralization would certainly reduce the probability that any scientist might betray the true intentions of the project to invasive beings.

If my prediction proves to be correct, then I anticipate that this elf may be slow to trust any being and might exhibit some form of paranoia. We must take care to create an environment of safety if her life is cast into the wind. Once we have given her some respite, we may meet with her on our own terms.

• • •

25 Reiselda, 635 C.I.

Our subject made her way to the local market in the morning to buy bread and berries. It was there that she made contact with the human recruiter as they blended into the world around them. Luckily, the secrecy of the crowd worked to our advantage, for it allowed us to consistently see and hear the two subjects as they masqueraded as a couple. We quickly learned some details that would certainly prove useful in the days to come. The scientist was known by the name of Rila, and she began to account for what she had seen in the laboratory.

"What have I done?" she said, attempting to cast off disturbing thoughts. "I have committed a horrible crime, and I want to end this nightmare. I want to leave this place!"

The agent attempted to comfort her, but Rila noticed that the personality of her acquaintance had changed in a manner that had made her feel worse. The meeting began to grow sour as suspicion turned into paranoia. Her concerns had not been without merit; her recruiter produced a small knife from his pocket. Rila exercised a defensive reflex as the blade clicked into position. In an instant, she produced her own knife and stabbed her associate in the chest. She removed the knife in one quick motion, but a state of shock soon settled over her as she stood there in disbelief over what she had done.

The shock soon turned to panic as a local female screamed. Rila dropped the knife and fled, which compelled Aegras and me to give chase, along with the local militia. In spite of the swarm of guards, Rila proved to be resourceful. She had done enough to create the illusion that she had vanished in the midst of the pursuit, which would leave the Telurians and the local constables in a state of bewilderment.

We tracked the movements of our subject as she developed a pattern of movement to shielded vantage points across the northern side of Tarilonis. As the bells rang to draw attention to her deed, Rila took refuge in an unoccupied residence away from the eyes of the local populace. Our appeals to reason would not do much to move the elf away from her state of panic, so we had no choice but to capture her. Our subject had given up with little resistance, save for an attempt to claw at Aegras as he restrained her.

I can only hope that she will be calm and more agreeable as time passes.

● ● ●

26 Reiselda, 635 C.I.

Rila had been silent for much of the time that I had overseen her, but her mind has not been shut away from the world. She responded to our initial attempts to feed her with glances of fear and worry over what had transpired. I suppose that she had to rummage through her mind to determine what she might say to Aegras and me, yet she was struggling to cope with the blood that had been spilled by the work of her hands. And so, we attempted to build a degree of trust through the provision of sustenance and some advisement as the day progressed.

"We want to help you," Aegras said. "You do not have to face this danger on your own."

At first, it had seemed that Rila would not respond to our persuasive efforts and that she would continue to withdraw from the world. As the hours passed, I think that she had grown to accept that we were no threat to her well-being. She later muttered that the Telurian Elite Guard would have failed to show her the mercy and understanding that we had given over the course of the day. Aegras contributed to those feelings by removing the restraints that we had placed upon her. As he turned to leave Rila for yet another time, our kin began to speak to us.

"Thank you," she said, struggling to smile. "You have been kind to me."

I must admit that I felt incredibly joyful when I overheard that short statement. She may not have conveyed information about the deeds of the enemy, but those questions will be answered with time and a sense of comfort that can be found in a relationship among friends, rather than strangers.

● ● ●

27 Reiselda, 635 C.I.

Rila began to open her mind and heart to us over the course of each meal today. The topics drifted with the passing of each moment, but much of our time had been spent in the examination of the course of her life. She expressed notions of guilt and anger over what she had done, for she felt that she had shamed the Avasyin family name. There was such desperation and misery in her demeanor that I began to sympathize with her plight, yet I felt that I needed to turn the discussion back to what we needed to know.

"You must understand me before I can help you," she said, polite but defiant. "I need you to know of the illusions that I have been facing ever since I was a child."

Rila had been born in the time when Thrakoth first sat upon his throne as a hero and chosen one of the people. However, it had been nothing more than an illusion carefully created by the institutions of power in the Telurian Empire. In some circles, the worship of their Lord rose to such levels that he had been seen as more than a human, elf, or dwarf. In essence, there was only one creed that existed within the walls of the enemy:

Obey and be rewarded. Disobedience is death.

Rila had never seen the darker side of the powers that kept her safe until the war had begun. Those who ruled under Thrakoth made certain that the disloyal would disappear into the night. She and her sons were conscripted into a cult of personality that would begin to break with supposed desertion and death. The family had been shamed in the eyes of an omniscient government, but Rila had begun to suspect that the real shame was in serving a faceless monster. The discovery of the lies and manipulation of her fellows would only serve to turn her against the Telurian Empire at great risk to her own life.

"I hope that my sons can come home to me in this new life," Rila said, distracted by thought and memory. "I want to see their faces and have them know that their nightmare is over."

It was in this moment that I had begun to see Rila as a being that yearned to be free of the shackles that had been placed upon her at the time of her birth. In addition, our discussion placed a certain emphasis upon my own failures. There is a difference between a people that would blindly serve a grand design and a people that are fooled and forced to choose between a horrible choice and a grave one.

I hope that I can garner the wisdom to discern the difference from this point forward.

• • •

28 Reiselda, 635 C.I.

My brother went out to gather more information and found the town to be stirring with news of the Telurian response to what Rila had done. Our new friend had been right to eliminate the human male who had offered to take her to safety in the west. In spite of his initial appearance as an agent of the sister republics, rumors had spread that he was either a Telurian agent or a close associate. While the identity of the enemy was essential to making appropriate decisions, it was not the most critical news that Aegras revealed to us.

Rila is being hunted by the locals and their new overlords for the crime of murder, but we presume that this is a pretext that will allow for the Telurians to eliminate any threats to their dominion over the city. The increasing patrols would hamper our movements through Tarilonis, but they may eventually make their secretive laboratories more visible to us. The desire to protect their research would be conveniently fulfilled in the ensuing chaos. In the fantasies outlined by the enemy horde, the Marshal would win the favor of Thrakoth and the progress toward the final triumph of the Telurian Empire would begin in earnest.

I do not know if Thrakoth possesses additional laboratories across the continent, but our success might allow us to find and destroy the other assets that the enemy has constructed. We will not be able to carry out such an undertaking on our own.

• • •

29 Reiselda, 635 C.I.

Our observation of the enemy met with some success as we moved through the city. Rila directed us to utilize a series of landmarks to find the Telurian laboratories, which confirmed the decentralized structure and secrecy of the Telurian effort. The two laboratories were thoroughly concealed, yet the addition of security to combat the threat posed by Rila had made them visible to Aegras and me. We have the strength to enter each facility on our own, but I fear that we shall not be able to disrupt or destroy what might be found in those secret lairs without awakening the entirety of the city.

Aegras, Rila, and I have developed a scheme to attack each of the Telurian laboratories. Rila knew what we were to find in each location, but it will require an expenditure of several days in order to bring our efforts to a full realization.

"I had been stationed in the abandoned council hall in the western portion of the city, which is where we conducted much of our research," she said. "That station had been separated from an underground lair that lies along the eastern bank of the river. That is where I uncovered the truth behind our experiments."

We found each laboratory in a measure of time befitting the description put forth by our defector. My brother and I decided to maintain a sense of distance from our prey for the time being. The Telurians had resolved to protect their research into the arts of war at any cost, so we must find a way to fight them on our terms.

● ● ●

30 Reiselda, 635 C.I.

I took responsibility for the Council Hall; the open structure and many shadows would be essential for the completion of a raid. However, the addition of reinforcements in past days has rendered my target much less open to an offensive movement. There are too many areas that the Telurians have sealed, preventing my entry unless I can provide a proper distraction. Thankfully, my dear telepath has proven to be most resourceful in his contribution to our schemes.

Aegras learned of the troubles that I would be facing and spent the day gathering supplies. When I found him in our hideout, he had begun to construct a series of pellets designed for the purposes of illusion and misdirection. The addition of several chemicals would serve to intensify the power of each smoke pellet. We would not know of their true strength without the promise of a successful test.

Aegras and I ventured into an alley just as the sun began to cross the horizon, taking great care to remain unseen. Aegras had exercised good sense in the choice to make our test look like a common trash fire, which creates a convenient means to mask our intentions even though a thick smoke might billow into the sky. There is little to say of what transpired there, save for that we had garnered a unique weapon that can cloud the vision and impede the breathing of our prey.

"It will be difficult for the enemy to notice us with no hope of sight," Aegras said. "Unfortunately, I was able to produce a mere six pellets with the supplies that I could salvage, so you should not rely upon them."

I felt no worry with the news that Aegras had given to me. The tricks that he concocted would render me a force of the natural world and instill fear and panic in those that oppose me. We have agreed to further the development of our scheme. Patience and cunning may yet eliminate the need to employ such trickery.

● ● ●

CHAPTER EIGHTEEN

31 Reiselda, 635 C.I.

Our observation of the enemy strongholds has revealed no major weakness in their defense. The guards change at intervals throughout the day and night, yet such processes are resolved in an instant. The character of these elites seem to be the most exemplary of the whole of the Telurian horde. They will not be distracted by any event that we can muster. Aegras and I believe that our efforts will require at least one direct confrontation before we may dwell in the shadows once more.

The cover of darkness appears to be our best chance for survival and success in undermining such destructive power while avoiding the problems that Aegras had raised this morning. In essence, my dear brother wondered if any of the Telurian scientists were as agreeable as Rila had been in days past. If such beings exist, then he and I have begun to consider the warring interests involved in this mess along with the possible spoilage of our minds.

"I believe that we have never before encountered a time when the line between innocence and guilt has been so thin," Aegras told me as he pondered our future. "I think that the light of the moon shall give us the means to avoid this dilemma, which our friends and allies may then utilize in order to create a critical advantage."

I am struggling to cope with the possible futures that may arise from our actions in this time and place. There are so many dangers and wonders that can be found in any road that might be chosen. And so, I find my mind wandering between doom and peace as we prepare for tomorrow night, but I know that the truth is not quite as simple as I might think.

● ● ●

6 Nemali, 635 C.I.

I do not think that I shall ever recall the full breadth of the horrors that Aegras encountered in that underground hovel, for he has not been willing to speak of what he had found there. Our connection provided a piece of insight over what had transpired in those halls. After a time, it became the place that the abductees were taken and experimented upon, resulting in the images that Thrakoth had cast across the known world. To the detriment of his mind, my dear brother had also encountered those who survived the tortures. Each and every one of them cried out in misery and begged for death, which was a comfort that Aegras felt moved to provide once he had eliminated those that opposed him.

I can tell that it had affected him deeply, for he has not yet returned to any semblance of normal behavior. The little sleep that he could muster was marred by the sights that we had both envisioned. In the light of day, he has become quiet and reflective as we continue our ride to the west, initially resisting my attempts to remove the doubt and dismay clouding his mind. His defenses would not last as I reached across his mind, forcing him to make his feelings known.

"I fear that Thrakoth means to be a merciless and cruel tyrant over a wasteland," Aegras wondered, looking upon me for the first time in several days. "How do we carry on in the face of such an atrocity of a being?"

I could glimpse the disgust and rage that had taken hold of my brother. He had to force himself to remain calm and prevent an unwarranted outburst.

"The only way to carry on is to end his reign of terror, dear brother," I replied. "With that said, I do think that he shall never be able to unleash those weapons upon the world. We now know too much about what he had done across the continent."

That statement appeared to give my dear brother an infusion of hope. After a time, I believe that he shall see his troubles cease due to the extraordinary value of the information that we are about to give to the sister republics.

● ● ●

7 Nemali, 635 C.I.

The former Council Hall of Tarilonis had become quite devoid of life on the night of our raid, save for the disciplined guards that haunted my path at every turn. The usage of stealth soon became an exercise in patience as I monitored the patrols and committed them to memory, using the passage of time as a means to quietly kill or incapacitate every being that might oppose me. The sudden disappearance of the patrolling guards quickly alerted the six that remained out of my grasp, prompting them to investigate. They adopted a defensive stance with their repeaters and advanced to the place where they thought I had hidden from sight. They had been completely wrong.

I sprang into action and rushed the elites from their flank. They turned to face my attack with the speed that I had expected. Any hope that they might have had of victory had disappeared with a single smoke pellet. In mere seconds, my opposition had been laid at my feet by the work of the blade.

I emerged from the smoke with the freedom to move about the exterior of the halls at will. No alarm had been raised in response to my intrusion. The same statement could not be made once the sun rose over the city. My time to act was running short. In the hopes of returning to some semblance of secrecy, I made my entrance into the Council Halls by climbing up the railings that lead to the central balcony.

It was when I ventured inside that the most unsettling events of the night would occur.

● ● ●

8 Nemali, 635 C.I.

I gained entry into the halls through an open passage that had been stretched along the top of an open venue of theory and discussion. With the light of candles as my aid, I could see a variety of equations and calculations far beyond my ken. It was a remarkable clash between the promise of science and the dark intent that the Telurians had levied against those in the west. I could only pay attention to the writings for a time, for I became frozen with fear by the gravest of appearances in the center of the laboratory.

Thrakoth was there on that night. Thankfully, my enemy had not noticed my presence under the cover of the darkness above. He seemed to have focused his mind upon another task. A scientist was escorted into the room through the lone set of double doors and gracefully bowed to his lord and master. The entire exchange seemed almost amicable upon first glance, but I believe that the elf felt utterly dominated in the presence of his overlord.

"I trust that your research is progressing as planned," Thrakoth said.

"Yes, my Lord. Our testing with live subjects has been more successful than we ever hoped. The only issues at hand are matters of constructing the explosive."

"You shall have all of the resources that you desire with the approach of spring."

"Thank you, my Lord."

"Remember the grand design in all of your efforts, young one," Thrakoth concluded, pointing at his subject. "I will be watching."

I began to harden my mind as I observed from the passages above. Thrakoth and his trusted scientist finished their discussion, and I became so paralyzed by the possible regret of letting the enemy leave unscathed. As I minded my every step, I drew and raised my two sidearms with the thought that one strike might end the misery and pain that had been inflicted upon us all.

The anticipation of a future in those precious moments would soon be halted by the realization that Thrakoth was more powerful than I had possibly imagined—he had seemingly vanished into the air.

The enemy had the power to project his being and thoughts across the vast expanse of this world, demonstrating that an end to this war was yet beyond our grasp. I had to cast the thought of easy revenge from my mind and focus on the matter at hand. There was a vast wealth of knowledge below me that had to be stolen or burned before the Telurians could ever make use of it. Thankfully, the disappearance of the one that I could not kill provided an opportunity to retrieve answers from those who remained in the expansive study. The scientist and his comrades knew many secrets that would be of use to the sister republics.

The only thought that impeded my strike was of how I might convince them.

● ● ●

9 Nemali, 635 C.I.

My quarrel with the scientist and his guards began as I had expected. After the elf concluded his report to Thrakoth, he made a retreat to his quarters while the soldiers lit his path. The relative absence of other people in the hall at such a late hour allowed me to stalk my prey with ease, for it was quite easy to determine the location of an oncoming enemy through the attunement of the five senses.

I minded my every movement as I followed them throughout the makeshift laboratory. The path was short and lacked any form of danger, save for when I occasionally sought shelter from the sight of another patrol. It had seemed to be such an easy feat to make my way to my quarry, yet my troubles intensified when another guard approached with news that had made her quite nervous.

"I am not able to find the gate keepers," the human female said, looking to her brethren. "They were supposed to switch positions on the patrol and they are late. They are never late."

"I will not have this elite guard fail in the duty that our Lord has prescribed," the scientist replied, annoyed at the thought of negligence and incompetence. "Find them."

The orders of my prey would never be fulfilled, for I thought it to be the opportune time to strike. The darkness of the corridor had left my enemy with no defense against the force of my abductions. The female that had noticed my efforts on the exterior of these halls was the first to be silenced at the point of a knife. Her sudden disappearance prompted an investigation from the remainder of those present, yet the simple distraction of a shattered bottle allowed me to separate and slay them. The loyalist would not be the last one to die in this battle of confusion and secrecy; he had taken up arms along with his comrades to face me.

With the fall of the Telurians, I ventured into the quarters of the First Councilor and found the treasures needed to save so many from doom. The elf that I had slain possessed pieces of information that pointed to the creation of laboratories across the known world. The most important and secretive details were written in a form of code. I do not have the ability to uncover the secrets within the diaries and papers on my own, so I can think of no better option other than to enlist the aid of our spies.

And so, I obtained all of the information that I could possibly carry away from Tarilonis. The rest of the paper and wood proved to be easy kindling for a fire that would consume the entire building. I could not pause to think of the implications of this victory. The ringing of alarm bells and the shout of oncoming aid for the survivors gave me reason to find Aegras and Rila, and we fled the city with all haste.

• • •

10 Nemali, 635 C.I.

I suspect that we have broken free from the grasp of the enemy once more, for there has been no sign of their hunting parties for the past two days. It is a welcome relief from the pressure that had been placed upon us since we had removed ourselves from Tarilonis. The Telurians had deployed expert trackers to counter our every deception through the lands of Callista, which left us with very few means to disappear into the wilderness.

Fortunately, the ingenuity and cunning of my dear brother had proven to be an admirable match for the best that Thrakoth had to offer, but it came with the price of some of our best equipment. In the days following our flight, Aegras began to utilize his arcane skills for the construction of a pellet that had been larger and more dangerous than any craft he had previously attempted. It is for this reason that he demanded that I keep away from him. He finally explained his scheme after a hard day of riding and work.

"It is the infusion of the powder of our ammunition and the essence of fire," Aegras said, holding the assembled weapon with great care.

This new construction had come in the shape of a modestly sized egg, pulsing with a strange crimson glow. It had seemed peculiar that an object of such small proportions could relieve us of our burden, but I placed the trust in my brother above such an odd thought. The gifts that he now held within his mind were a great testament to the power of evolution and family.

We made our way to an abandoned home, giving our foes the perception of desperation and fear. In the eyes of the enemy, it would appear as if we were running out of food and desired the warmth of a bed for the night through the trickery of wandering movement and spent ammunition. Our long and visible journey ensured that a good portion of our hunters would eventually be present at that little cabin in the wild, which would set the second portion of our scheme into motion.

We did not possess the resources needed to construct an elaborate illusion, so we resolved to make the enemy think that it would be easy to strike the cabin. The closure of curtains and illumination of small oil lamps were all we could muster in defense of our path into the west, but it would prove more than satisfactory as we observed the cabin from the cover of the trees to the north and west.

The hunters made their appearance with stealth and

cunning, bending down to analyze our initial tracks with the accuracy that we had come to expect from such feared adversaries. They quietly approached the cabin by moving between several obstacles in the southern reaches of the area. The small branches and twigs snapped under their every step as they crept forward, struggling to avoid alarming us of their presence until they had surrounded the cabin.

The best of the hunters took their positions along each door and quietly turned the handles. The passage of several seconds had given us pause as the hunters failed to move into the structure, but the sudden closure of the doors and shouts of panic would soon overtake our senses.

"Explosive!" one hunter screamed. "Make for the trees!"

In an instant, they would know no more.

• • •

CHAPTER NINETEEN

16 Nemali, 635 C.I.

I felt as though a great weight had been lifted from our shoulders as we passed into the reclaimed territories of Callista earlier today, but our journey could not continue without further obstacles. We were greeted by a Callistan patrol that had not known of our struggle over the past month. They were compelled to detain us until their ride was completed. Out of the fear that we were spies for the enemy, they had said little of their path through the land. Rila, Aegras, and I thought it best to comply with their requests as we rode to the south and west. In return, our brothers and sisters treated us with what care they could muster, healing the cuts and bruises that we had sustained on our path.

Aegras and I were escorted to a moderately sized homestead and stripped of each weapon in our possession. The humans approached the task with great care. I could see that they feared us in spite of our cooperation and friendly demeanor. As our weapons were bundled and carried away, we were placed in a small chamber—our home for a day or two. Our allies had afforded no luxury to us, save for the allowance of two candles, a jar of ink, and a quill. I take solace in their allowance for my writing, as I have hidden the intelligence that I shall give to our government between these pages. These materials will never leave my presence.

● ● ●

17 Nemali, 635 C.I.

We waited for many hours in the early morning before our allies allowed us to be free of our confines. We were escorted to our morning meal in the presence of the Sergeant at Arms. This dominating being had been chosen to investigate our story. The human had begun to feast upon a lavish breakfast of meat and eggs. He made no effort to give his name to Aegras or me.

"If you do not tell me the truth, then you will be taken to prison," he warned, picking at his eggs with a fork. "I trust that my statement was clear?"

We nodded our heads.

"We were pursued on an errand of secrecy. My name is Helisah, and the name of my brother is Aegras. May I ask where we are?"

"Forty kilometers to the north of Arduth. Are you traveling to that city?"

"The governor knows of our identities. I request that you send a messenger to her so that we may be released."

"And what can you say of the female who accompanied you?"

"Her name is Rila. She is a scientist who came to our aid. She seeks asylum from the Telurian Empire."

"Very well. I shall arrange for a letter to be sent as soon as we are able," the Sergeant said, waving us away. "You shall have our answer in due time."

We would wait for a long time to be free of our detainment, but we passed the time by overhearing the tales of our allies as they stood watch over our door. It was a welcome relief to hear tales of life and sanity over the dust and echoes of the past. We would simply listen and feel content with the knowledge that our trials were worth the cost, leading up to the pleasant sight of the Sergeant at Arms as the sun set over the land.

The governor intervened on our behalf. We shall be free to leave at dawn.

• • •

18 Nemali, 635 C.I.

I feel some small sense of pride when I say that the people of Arduth have survived and prospered since the day that it was liberated with blood and tears. The uncertainty that had been felt in those early hours had carried on for a time, but the agreeable weather and proficient leadership gave the people a chance to build up their lives again. We had even noticed that the Callistan government and private businesses had seen it fit to begin construction on new buildings.

Aegras and I were welcomed with little fanfare, save for an acknowledgement from the few that had known or heard of us. If I am an honest elf, those quiet demonstrations of a connection to other beings are all I ever need in my life. It has long provided a sense of understanding and compassion when the world may seem to be shrouded in confusion and ambiguity, which gave us some small sense of relief from what we had endured over the past month. The arrival of letters addressed to Aegras and me lifted our minds even further, for they brought tidings of love and family from the east and the west.

Aegras had been given three letters from the Raiders and a small bottle that was filled to the brim with an unrecognizable elixir. I could feel a sense of happiness overwhelm my dear telepath in that moment, for he had grown fond of his kindred in a way that mirrors my own emotions. He proceeded to read the second letter in silence. I could sense that the fondness that he had felt had escalated into feelings of love and caring. I did not venture any further with our connection in the hopes of uncovering the source behind these feelings, for I had no desire to think of such matters when the one that I love had provided a bounty of affection.

I received four letters from Fasti later in the evening. They had been written over a long span of time as he marched to the east. He had seemed overwhelmed by the thought of our reunion and running to the nearest bed in order to take back the many days that we had sacrificed for the sake of the future. The feelings that were expressed in these letters had ignited the hunger and yearning within my mind once more. This well of emotion did not come from the mere desire for sexual fulfillment; it came from the notion that he had touched the entirety of my being.

• • •

19 Nemali, 635 C.I.

The governor had been swift to meet with us in the early

hours of this day, but it was not to exchange pleasantries. She wished to know of the plans of the enemy in order to feed information back to the government in Nuveia. The threat of a weapon of doom sparked grave worry among the few that knew of these secrets. Fortunately, the political figures of the sister republics managed to keep this danger a secret from the people that they had sworn to serve. The intelligence agents and the attuned followed without question, concealing any panic among their ranks, for the benefit of all.

The governor became quite dismayed over the course of our meeting, for we had no information that might allay the fears of those in power. The revelation that Thrakoth had distributed the process of researching and building the weapon across an entire continent did little to bring the room to calm. In truth, it caused an outburst on the part of our host.

"One explosive would be enough to doom us to a new dark age, and you expect me to think that these little matters are important without proof?" she fumed.

"If we have hope of victory, then every detail shall be of grave importance," I countered, sternly disapproving of her anguish. "This particular piece of information suggests that it will be easy to thwart the design of our enemy."

"You think that these words will be enough to convince the chancellors?"

"Yes."

"Good," she concluded, calmly. "You will have time to say as much when they visit in two days."

In spite of their knowledge and trust in us, the approach of the most powerful beings in the allied governments would hold little weight if we did not have enough information to back our claims of a weakness in the enemy. In truth, the decentralization of the Telurian research program provided more advantages than hindrances. The laboratories and facilities would be harder to raze, but the elaborate nature of this endeavor meant that every disruption would purchase a precious amount of time. In the wake of each transaction, the passage of time might offer us a certain degree of strength and sanity that would make these outbursts of fear into a relic of the past.

On a personal level, I would settle for a degradation to a mere annoyance, if it should please nature and my own mind.

The salvaged intelligence has since been given off to a number of trusted agents stationed in Arduth. After a time, these fellows of the shadow allowed us to join them, in the hope of adding to the little knowledge that they had of this weapon of essence. Aegras and I spent the entire day and much of the night giving an account of any minute detail that we might have noticed. Such clues might lead us to break the code of the enemy and know every secret and craft they hold dear.

● ● ●

20 Nemali, 635 C.I.

Aegras and I continued to labor towards some form of progress with our kindred, but the secret ledgers proved to be a formidable challenge. The intelligence agents theorized that there might be some sort of key to break the apparent nonsense that clouded the paper. Yet the combinations that we tried have failed to produce a result. The arrival of more skilled beings made certain that we would never want for new hypotheses. While very few of those thoughts would befit such secretive research, this exchange of ideas created a mindful focus on our task, cutting through the frustration and confusion.

We were certain that we would find the truth, but the many hours that we spent staring upon pieces of paper would take their toll. Aegras and I left to seek out our evening meal with many of our fellows, and there was no discussion of mathematics or the Telurian Empire. The day yielded nothing more than aching heads and plenty of spent parchment, so my kin thought it best to think of slices of roasted chicken and honey beer. The rations would more than suffice to slake our hunger and thirst, yet Aegras had become enraptured in thought as he ate.

What if it is a word, dear sister? Aegras thought. *It is a pattern hidden in plain sight.*

The musings of my dear brother provided a sense of clarity at that late hour, for we had found a unique solution that would provide the Telurians with an equal measure of protection and convenience. We kept our thoughts hidden until we were finished with our meal and the mental stress of the day had been lifted.

We returned to our working chambers with a renewed vigor. Aegras presented the concept convincingly enough to allow for a new period of labor, yet the sun had set in our absence from our working chambers. Our thoughts were to be tested by the light of the candle as night drifted over the land.

We began with our thoughts on what the enemy valued most in all of the world, building a list of words out of the rumors and experiences that had surfaced in this fight. The agents had spoken of how the enemy had reflected upon family and their own culture, envisioning a new world by following the will of their Lord. The thought of the designs that Thrakoth had planned for the world would take shape from my participation in the discussion, prompting my immediate assignment of that accursed word as our first task.

We set our minds upon moving through the word in order to isolate the alphabetical pattern and followed with a movement through every page that we could muster at such a late hour. In time, our suspicions had been proven correct with the successful translation of two lines, revealing that the enemy had associated the towns of Meldrais and Eldrahin with their weapons. The enemy had left no indication of the host nation for these laboratories, but I believe that Chancellor Valiri will be able to come to our aid in finding a solution.

● ● ●

21 Nemali, 635 C.I.

We have uncovered much of what the enemy had planned for their research program, yet there are allusions to further discoveries within these documents that we have not even begun to fathom. In spite of an incomplete understanding of the enemy, we garnered enough information from these ledgers to make further moves against Thrakoth and his designs. With the razing of their laboratories in Tarilonis, the Telurians would have to make due with twelve major scientific stations that were spread out across the known world. Our kin theorized that the complexity of this weapon would allow for the discovery of additional secret hovels and stolen buildings.

However, the acknowledgement of these possibilities were of little concern when compared to the thought that there may be traitors in our midst. The enemy had distributed their efforts to the cities of Suva and Teldanil within the Fiean Republic, which alarmed the Callistan and Fiean spies who once occupied these chambers. The appearance of an internal enemy would be damaging to the confidence of the sister republics, whether these conspirators were selling information for money or plotting in secret. Therefore, it was deemed necessary and prudent to recommend that this new danger should be destroyed through a progression of unfortunate events, if only to maintain the safety and sanity of all.

● ● ●

22 Nemali, 635 C.I.

The chancellors were greeted with a strong fanfare from the moment that their carriages entered the city. The arrival of these two beings had been cast as a symbol that hope was not lost in the midst of war. The entirety of the local population seemed to be out in the streets to observe the passing caravan, if only to cheer on these political leaders and offer flowers to the escorting soldiers. The arrival of the press intensified the magnitude of these small gestures, for they would soon carry the message of this day across the known world in the face of Thrakoth and the

Telurian Empire.

A number of people would follow the chancellors to the town square, gathering in an orderly fashion to hear Chancellor Valiri speak of the path of the sister republics. It was nothing more than political rhetoric designed to provoke the people into a state of fervor, but I had forgotten how gifted a politician can be with a dominating presence and oratory skill. In an instant, Valiri commanded the crowd with a soaring display of what he thought that Arduth had represented, culminating in a statement that would not be forgotten.

"For all of this time, a free people have lived in fear that a monster would take their lives, their fortunes, and their honor," Chancellor Valiri said with great force. "I ask you on this day to take back what is yours and fear no one!"

The crowd gave a roar of approval that lasted through the clasping of hands with his Fiean counterpart. After a time, the two leaders turned away from an adoring populace and enter the offices of the governor. It was here that our most secret endeavor would begin in earnest.

● ● ●

The news of another blow to the efforts of our enemy was met with little satisfaction from the chancellors, for they felt that the war would fall from our grasp with the passage of time. They agreed that the deployment of a weapon of this magnitude would cause widespread panic across the sister republics, utterly destroying the ability of the alliance to wage war on their own terms.

"The appearance of this weapon will create a state of utter paralysis across the known world," Chancellor Valiri remarked. "Let it be known that you shall have the full support of my government in finding and eliminating this new threat."

"The Fiean Republic will lend all that it can muster as well," Chancellor Adello stated, looking over his report. "My only concerns are the missing pieces of information."

Our fellows told of how three of the Telurian laboratories appeared to be outside of the known world, yet this assertion would be swiftly corrected by the words of Chancellor Valiri. He had reviewed the secretive ledger and found the town of Cardasgir to be within the Dalarian Republic. The thought of deceit and betrayal immediately took shape in our minds, but I think another circumstance clouded this matter even further.

What if the Dalarian government did not know of this secret?

According to Chancellor Valiri, the settlement was relatively isolated from the rest of Dalaria during the frigid winters of the north. It is quite plausible that these circumstances could lead to affairs of subterfuge and extortion at a time when the survival of the people would be of the greatest concern. In time, the agents of the enemy would find it easy to take the town for their own ends, putting down a token resistance from time to time without mercy.

"We have no desire to start a fight with the Dalarians," Chancellor Adello said. "However, we must be decisive in our efforts as a new season draws near."

"I will place spies into the Dalarian government. We must discover why the enemy has taken shelter there," Chancellor Valiri replied.

Aegras and I saw fit to engage in this task, raising our hands as the gaze of our Chancellor came to us. He had been quite pleased with our insistence to cross the seas to the Dalarian Republic, yet my dear brother felt that his words were required to express our resolve.

"We will go," Aegras asserted.

"Excellent," Chancellor Valiri replied. "I am confident that your skills will be of great value in this venture."

After a time, a clear vision of dealing with the enemy was formed and put into action. The agents of the sister republics would be placed near each laboratory in preparation to strike at the heart of the Telurian Empire. Our attacks were planned to be conducted at a rapid pace, for we could not allow the enemy to disappear and continue their research elsewhere. Our efforts in Cardasgir would become the single exception to these orders, due to the discretion that would be necessary for our success. The Dalarians would never know that we were within their borders until we had discovered the truth of their allegiance and their apparent connection to the Telurian Empire.

● ● ●

EPILOGUE

THE DARKNESS

Kei ferani evudia noi veruni.

The statement stands on merit.

- Celrohin Evyndein, 3rd Foreign Minister of the
Fiean Republic

CHAPTER TWENTY

5 Lunedil, 635 C.I.

It feels wondrous to witness the sprouting of new life from the darkness of the winter, especially when we are able to see such feats of nature while under the protection of my family. Aegras and I were made welcome in the hideout of the Raiders with offerings of ale and games, and our brothers and sisters had many stories with an equal fill of laughter and tragedy to share in those halls. In the telling of these tales, the past week has filled me with the joy that I had missed since Gialle and Duustan were taken from us.

I still think of my brethren and the pain that I felt on the fields of Arduth, yet the end of their lives is only a shadow and a thought in the back of my mind. I feel that an example of their lives can be found in this place, for they were an inseparable pair that had never wasted a single moment. I swear that this passion for life and liberty is the dearest memory that I shall ever have of them.

In the morning, Aegras and I will depart for our meeting with the crew of the CS *Nevani*. According to Chancellor Valiri, the ship has been ordered to sail into the territorial waters of the

Dalarian Republic under the colors of a trading vessel, conveniently obscuring our activities until we reach the shore.

● ● ●

6 Lunedil, 635 C.I.

The crew of the *Nevani* paid little attention to us as we came aboard; they were quite accustomed to moving agents and cargo across the seas. The Quartermaster welcomed us in the name of his Captain, showing Aegras and me to a set of bunk beds set aside for the shadowy figures that would board this vessel. The man spoke little in those moments, but he explained that this was on the orders of a Captain who held secrecy as the highest prize.

Aegras and I were left to listen to the crew and the water as we departed on our journey across the northern seas. We passed the time with a pair of board games that had been placed in our cabin, exercising our minds for the sake of avoiding the boredom that would come with waiting for our dinner. We traded dominance over the game board many times over those hours of play, yet we became distracted by outside forces and created tactical mistakes. We blamed the waves or the sound of the crew, but neither my brother nor I had been willing to admit that there was another force to blame for our mistakes.

There was a darkness that had been at work in the back of our minds. I do not know how we had come upon this disturbance, but I could feel that it was reaching out and touching my consciousness in a manner designed not to frighten or control me, but to observe my thoughts and activities. There was no power that Aegras and I could wield for the removal of this spell, but I am certain that our free will is not in jeopardy.

• • •

7 Lunedil, 635 C.I.

We had eaten our morning meal and returned to our quarters when the darkness returned to our minds. This disturbance had grown stronger with the passing of the night, taking hold over a greater portion of my mind. I could feel the power of each movement across my consciousness. I came to know that these disturbances were not from Thrakoth. The being that had been seeking us was one of far greater power, reaching out across a vast distance for reasons that I could not comprehend until it had taken utter control of our vision and hearing.

Aegras and I screamed in pain as successive visions swept across our sight. We saw lands and cities that were known to us across the entirety of their development, but this passage across time and space would soon be overtaken by the eyes and voice of a dominating being.

You travel on the path to war, Helisah and Aegras Almari. The sequence expands and the ends are many, yet I must know if you are a unifying force or the harbinger of our destruction.

• • •

Acknowledgements

This novel would not be complete without giving recognition to those who helped me to make it into something special.

Thank you to Josh Huff. Your attention to detail and dedication to the craft of editing gave me the push that I needed to polish this story to a mirror shine. You brought out the best in every hero, villain, and devious scheme that I wrote about.

Thank you to Hermann Kromer. Your creative vision and craftsmanship was the key behind the creation of an exceptional piece of cover art. Every time I look at it, it seems like I am looking through a window onto this new world of wonder.

Thank you to my father, mother, and my family. These characters might not have been born if we hadn't bought those books, seen those movies, and played those video games together.

Lastly, and perhaps most importantly, I want to thank you for reading this book. I can't wait to show you all the great stories that are to come.

www.ingramcontent.com/pod-product-compliance
Lightning Source LLC
Chambersburg PA
CBHW051241250626
47155CB00009B/3124